ABOVE SUSPICION . . . ?

"There's no doubt that Morgan has infiltrated the Guard at practically every level. From the bottom to the top. But for once we have a name. Morgan's bought himself a Guard Captain, someone so loyal and honourable as to be above suspicion."

"Tell me the name," said Hawk.

Linden swallowed hard, and looked briefly at Shire for support. "You're not going to like this, Hawk. I don't have any proof or evidence; this is just what I heard. I could be wrong."

"Just tell me the bloody name!"

"Fisher," said Linden. "Captain Isobel Fisher."

Ace Books by Simon R. Green

HAWK & FISHER
WINNER TAKES ALL
THE GOD KILLER
WOLF IN THE FOLD
GUARD AGAINST DISHONOR

THE BONES OF HAVEN
(coming in March)

HAWK & FISHER
GUARD AGAINST DISHONOR

SIMON R. GREEN

ACE BOOKS, NEW YORK

This book is an Ace original edition,
and has never been previously published.

GUARD AGAINST DISHONOR

An Ace Book / published by arrangement with
the author

PRINTING HISTORY
Ace edition / December 1991

ISBN: 0-441-31836-3

Ace Books are published by The Berkley Publishing Group,
200 Madison Avenue, New York, New York 10016.
The name "ACE" and the "A" logo
are trademarks belonging to Charter Communications, Inc.

PRINTED IN THE UNITED STATES OF AMERICA

10 9 8 7 6 5 4 3 2 1

1

Chacal

There are bad cities, there are worse cities; and then there's Haven.

By popular acclaim the vilest and most corrupt city in the Low Kingdoms, Haven in midwinter gleams purest white under falls of frozen snow, and its towers shine with frost and ice like pillars of crystal. But only from a distance. The snow on the ground is a dirty grey from the unceasing factory smoke, and grey-faced people trudge wearily through the snow-choked streets.

Seen up close, Haven is an ugly city, in more ways than one. Even in the early morning, when the killing cold grips the streets like a clenched fist, there is still no peace for the city. There are still deals to be made, conspiracies to be entered into, and blood to be spilled. Death is a way of life in Haven, and sudden violence the pulse of its narrow streets.

And only the city Guard, stretched to breaking point at the best of times, stands between the city and open, bloody chaos.

Hawk and Fisher, husband and wife and Captains in the city Guard, strode briskly down the crowded street towards Guard Headquarters, their prisoner scurrying along between them. Winter had finally come to Haven, despite everything

1

the city weather wizards could do, and the bitter air was several degrees below freezing. The street was ankle-deep in snow and slush, and thick icicles hung from every building. Roofs groaned under the weight of a week's accumulated snow, and the iron-grey sky promised more blizzards to come. But still people packed the street from end to end; men, women, and children jostling each other impatiently as they hurried to and from work. No one jostled Hawk and Fisher, of course. It wouldn't have been wise.

It was eight o'clock in the morning, but so dark that street lamps still burned at every corner, their amber glare doing little to dispel the gloom. Hawk hated the winter, and not just because the recent flu epidemic had hit the Guard badly and he and Fisher were working a double shift for the third day running. Winter meant hard times in Haven, and hardest of all for the poor and destitute. In every street, in every part of the city, there were bodies lying stiff and cold, caught out in the freezing night because they had nowhere else to go. They ended up in sheltered doorways, or huddled together under tarpaulins in back alleyways, sharing their meagre warmth as best they could. Every day the garbage squad made their rounds and hauled the bodies away, but there were always more. Hawk found a young girl once, curled in a tight little ball over a street grating. She couldn't have been more than five or six years old, and her staring eyes had frozen solid in her head. Hawk hated the winter, and sometimes he hated Haven too.

Captain Hawk was tall, dark-haired, and no longer handsome. A series of old scars ran down the right side of his face, and a black silk patch covered his right eye. He told lots of stories about how he got the scars, most of them contradictory. His thick furs and official black cloak made him look impressively bulky, but underneath his winter uniform he was lean and wiry rather than muscular, and building a stomach. He wore his shoulder-length hair loose, mostly to keep his ears warm, and kept it out of his vision with a plain leather headband. He'd only just turned thirty, but already there were streaks of grey in his hair. At first glance he seemed like just another bravo, a sword-for-hire already past his prime, but few people ever stopped at a first glance. There was something about Hawk, something cold and unyielding that gave even the most belligerent hardcase pause to think twice. On his right hip, Hawk carried a short-handled axe instead of a sword. He was very good with an axe. He'd had lots of practice.

Captain Isobel Fisher walked confidently at his side, echoing her partner's stance and pace with the naturalness of long companionship. She was tall, easily six feet in height, and her long blond hair fell to her waist in a single thick plait, weighted at the tip with a polished steel ball. She wore a battered and almost shapeless fur hat, pulled down low to protect her ears from the bitter cold. There was a rawboned harshness to her face, barely softened by her deep blue eyes and generous mouth. She was handsome rather than pretty, her gaze was cool and direct, and she didn't smile much. Sometime, somewhere in the past, something had scoured all the human weaknesses out of her, and it showed. She wore the same furs and cloak as Hawk, though with rather more grace and style. She wore a sword on her hip, and her skill with it was legendary, in a city not easily impressed by legends.

Hawk and Fisher, feared and respected by one and all as the toughest and most honest Guards in Haven. They had a lot of enemies, both inside and outside the Guard.

Their prisoner was a short, scrawny, harmless-looking man, wrapped in a long fur coat, topped off with a pair of fluffy earmuffs. His thinning black hair was plastered to his head with rather more grease than necessary, and he had a permanent scowl. Benny the Weasel was not a happy man.

"You're making a terrible mistake," he repeated for the tenth time, in what he imagined was an ingratiating tone. "Let's be reasonable about this."

"Sorry," said Hawk, without looking round. "I'm only reasonable at weekends. And Fisher doesn't believe in being reasonable. Says it's bad for her image."

"Right," said Fisher, glaring horribly at a nun who hadn't got out of her way fast enough.

"This is all a misunderstanding," said Benny doggedly. "I am a legitimate businessman."

Hawk snorted derisively. "Benny, you are a small-time villain who makes most of his money running a nasty little protection racket, advising local shopkeepers of all the awful things that might happen to them or their premises if they don't keep up the payments. Only this time you were dumb enough to do it in person, in front of Fisher and me. What's the matter, both your leg-breakers down with the flu?"

Benny sniffed. "You can't get good help these days. Look, I am an important figure in the community. I know my rights. I pay my taxes. Technically, you work for me."

"Then you should be pleased to be getting such value for your money," said Fisher. "We witnessed a crime and arrested the criminal on the spot. What more do you want?"

"You won't get away with this!" said Benny desperately. "I have friends. I have influence. You won't be able to make this charge stick. I'll be out on the streets again before you can blink!"

Hawk looked at him. "You know, Benny, you're starting to get on my nerves. Now, be a good fellow and shut your face or I'll have Fisher take you into the nearest dark alley and reason with you for a while."

Benny glanced at Fisher, and then looked quickly away when he discovered she was smiling at him. He'd heard about Fisher's idea of reasoning with people. If she did it where they lived, it tended to play hell with the furniture. Benny had second thoughts, and they walked the rest of the way in silence.

Guard Headquarters loomed up before them, a massive squat stone building with heavy oaken doors and arrow-slit windows. It had the look of a place constantly under siege, which wasn't far off the mark. Riots, hexes, and firebombings were a part of everyday life for the Headquarters, but no one had ever closed it down for more than a few hours. It had its own sorcerers, and everyone in the building went armed at all times, from the clerks to the Commanders. It took a lot to disrupt the Headquarters' even running, though last year's rash of possessions had come close.

The main doors were always open, but everyone knew that could change in a second if danger threatened. A long-established spell on the doors saw to that, and tough luck if anyone got in the way. A steady stream of people bustled in and out of the building as Hawk and Fisher approached with their prisoner. There was the usual mixture of Constables and the people helping them with their enquiries, along with anxious relatives searching for the recently arrested, and backstreet lawyers touting for business. And of course there were always those who'd come to the Guard for help, all with the same thinly disguised look of fear and desperation. Most people only went to the Guard when they'd tried everything else. The law was harsh and brutal, and weighted heavily in favour of the rich and powerful. There were Guards who were sympathetic, and would do what they could for those in real need, but for the most part the poor had no reason to trust the Guard. Like everything else in Haven, justice was for sale. Everyone had their price.

Everyone except Hawk and Fisher.

Benny thought fleetingly of making a run for it, then noticed that Fisher's hand was resting casually on the pommel of her sword, and quickly thought better of it. He sighed heavily, and accompanied Hawk and Fisher through the main doors and into the crowded lobby of Guard Headquarters. The wide, low-ceilinged room was packed from wall to wall, and the noise was deafening. Mothers and grandmothers sat in little groups against the walls, chatting and gossiping and keeping a watchful eye on their children as they scampered back and forth, getting in everyone's way. None of them had any real business at Headquarters, but the Guard let them stay. It was the only place in that area where small children could play safely. Besides which, the Guard Constables had found they could pick up a lot of useful information by casually listening in on the women's gossip.

Over by the booking desk in the centre of the lobby, a seething mob of people screamed and shouted and pleaded, together with much shedding of tears and beating of breasts, but the three desk Sergeants took it in their stride. They'd heard it all before. They nodded more or less sympathetically to worried relatives, glared at the lawyers, and got on with booking the various criminals as the Constables brought them forward, as though the utter bedlam around them was of absolutely no interest.

Hawk and Fisher made their way through the shifting mass of bodies by sheer determination and liberal use of their elbows. Hawk hammered on the desk with his fist until he got a Sergeant's attention, and then handed Benny over into his keeping. The Sergeant fixed him with a malicious grin.

"Well, well, what have we here? It's not often you grace us with your loathsome company, Benny. What did you do to upset Hawk and Fisher?"

"Nothing! I was just minding my own business . . ."

"Your business is illegal, Benny, and if you were stupid enough to do it in front of those two, you deserve everything that happens to you." He struck the large brass bell beside him, the sharp sound cutting cleanly through the surrounding babble, and a Constable came over to the desk and led Benny away. Hawk and Fisher watched them go, Benny the Weasel still loudly protesting his innocence.

"We won't be able to hold him, you know," said the desk Sergeant.

Fisher looked at him sharply. "Why the hell not? We'll both give evidence against him."

"It'll never come to trial," said the Sergeant. "Benny has friends, hard though that is to believe. The word will come down, and we'll have to let him go."

Fisher scowled. "Sometimes I wonder why we bother making arrests at all. These days, it seems practically every villain and thug we meet has connections with someone higher up. Or the judge gets bribed. Or the jury gets intimidated."

"That's Haven for you," said the Sergeant. "Hey, don't look at me. I just work here."

Fisher growled something indistinct, and allowed Hawk to pull her away from the desk. They elbowed their way back through the crowd, glaring down any objections, and found a place by the huge open fireplace to warm their hands and take a seat for a moment. They nodded amiably to the half-dozen Constables already there. None of them actually had any business that required their presence at Headquarters, but none of them were that keen to give up the nice warm lobby for the freezing cold outside. Hawk turned around and lifted his cloak to warm his backside at the fire. He smiled happily and looked out over the lobby.

A small group of whores, looking bright and gaudy and not a little chilly in their working finery, were waiting patiently to be booked, fined, and released so that they could get back to work as quickly as possible. Some politician or newspaper editor must have had a sudden attack of principles, or been leaned on by some pressure group, and declared loudly that Something Should Be Done about the rising tide of vice in Our Fair City. So the Guard made a big show of arresting whoever happened to be around at the time, the pimps paid the fines out of their petty cash, and business went on as usual. Hawk shrugged. It was none of his business. He nodded to a few familiar faces, and then tensed as one of the girls was viciously backhanded by her pimp. Hawk strode quickly over to them and dropped a heavy hand on the pimp's shoulder. The pimp spun round, knocking the hand away, and then froze as he realised who it was. He was young and muscular, with a ratty-looking moustache, dressed to the nines and proud of it. He studied Hawk warily.

"What do you want, Captain? I'm clean."

"You wouldn't be clean if you washed every day with sulphuric acid. You are a pimp, Sebastian, the lowest of the low, and I know you of old. I thought I warned you about maltreating your girls."

"Me? Hurt my girls?" said Sebastian, looking around him as though to invite the world to witness his harassment. "I love my girls like sisters! Who sees they always have nice clothes to wear, and looks after all their needs? They're like family to me, all my girls. They just need a little firm guidance from time to time, that's all."

"Your associate and business partner, that nasty little thug Bates, is currently awaiting trial for 'firmly guiding' one of your girls by slashing her face with a razor," said Hawk. "I know you, Sebastian; I know you and all your nasty little ways. And if I discover you've been firmly guiding any of your girls again, I shall be annoyed with you. You do remember what happened when I got annoyed with Bates, don't you?"

The pimp nodded reluctantly. "He's making good progress. He should be out of hospital soon."

"Really? I must be losing my touch. Keep your hands off the girls, Sebastian. Or I'll tie your fingers in knots."

Sebastian smiled and nodded as though it hurt him, and disappeared into the crowd. Hawk watched him go, nodded politely to the whores, who ignored him, and made his way back to the fire. Fisher was down on her knees, playing with a few children too young to be afraid of a Guard's uniform. Hawk watched for a while, smiling gently. Isobel was good with kids. They'd talked about having children of their own more than once, but somehow it never seemed to be the right time.

The crowd suddenly erupted in shouts and screams, and backed quickly away as a prisoner who'd broken away from his escort lashed about him with a knife he'd somehow kept hidden. He grabbed for one of the children by Fisher, obviously intending to use the child as a hostage. Fisher glanced round and back-elbowed him viciously in the groin. She rose unhurriedly to her feet as the prisoner hunched forward over his pain, then rabbit-punched him. He collapsed and lay still. Fisher kicked the knife away from his hand and went back to playing with the children. Two Constables dragged the unconscious prisoner away.

Hawk decided regretfully that they'd killed about as much time as they could get away with, and they ought really to get back to the job. They were barely halfway through their second shift. He tried concentrating on all the overtime they were racking up, but it didn't help. His feet were numb, his forehead still ached from the cold, and his back was killing him. Hawk hated the winter. He collected Fisher, waved goodbye to the kids and their unresponsive mothers, and strode resignedly out into the waiting cold. And the first thing he saw was Benny the Weasel shivering in a borrowed cloak as he tried unsuccessfully to hail a sedan chair. Hawk and Fisher looked at each other, and strolled casually over to join him. Benny saw them coming, and clearly thought about making a run for it, before better sense took over. He drew himself up to his full five foot six and tried to brazen it out.

"Benny," said Hawk reproachfully, "what do you think you're doing out here?"

"They let me go," said Benny quickly, his eyes darting from Hawk to Fisher and back again. "All the charges have been dropped. That's official. Told you I had friends."

Hawk and Fisher stepped forward, took an elbow each, and carried Benny kicking and protesting into the nearest back alley. As soon as they put him down, he tried to bolt, but Hawk snagged him easily and slammed him against the wall, just hard enough to rattle his eyes and put a temporary stop to any complaints. Hawk brought his face close to Benny's, and fixed him with his single cold eye.

"No one walks when we bring the charges, Benny. Not ever. I don't care what kind of friends you've got, you are guilty as hell and you're going to stand trial."

"They won't accept your evidence," said Benny desperately. "The judge will let me off. You'll see."

Hawk sighed. "You're not getting the message, Benny. If we let you walk, all the other scum will start thinking they can get away with things. And we can't have that, can we? So you are going to walk back into Headquarters, make a full confession, and plead guilty. Because if you don't, Fisher and I will take turns thinking up horrible things to do to you."

"They won't convict me on just a confession."

"Then you'd better be sure to provide plenty of corroborative evidence. Hadn't you?"

Benny looked at Hawk's implacable face and then glanced at Fisher. She had a nasty-looking skinning knife in her hand,

and was calmly paring her nails with it. Benny studied the knife with fascinated eyes and swallowed hard. Right then, all the awful stories he'd heard about Hawk and Fisher seemed a lot more believable than they had before. Hawk coughed politely to get his attention, and Benny almost screamed.

"Benny . . ."

"I think I'd like to confess, please, Captain Hawk."

"You do realise you don't have to?"

"I want to."

"Legally, you're not bound to do so . . ."

"Please, let me confess! I want to! Honestly!"

"Good man," said Hawk, standing back from him. "It's always refreshing to meet a citizen who believes in honesty and justice. Now, get in there and start talking while we're still in a good mood."

Benny ran out of the alleyway and back into Guard Headquarters. Fisher smiled and put away her knife. The two Guards left the alley and made their way unhurriedly down the street, heading back to their beat in the Northside.

The Northside was the rotten heart of Haven, where all that was bad in the city came to the surface, like scum on poisoned wine. Crime and corruption and casual evil permeated the Northside, where every taste and trade was catered to. Various gangs of drug dealers fought running battles over lucrative territories, ruthlessly cutting down any innocent bystanders who got in the way. Spies plotted treason behind shuttered windows, and many doors opened only to the correct whispered password. Sweatshops and crowded slum tenements huddled together under broken street lamps, and the smoke from local factories hung permanently on the air, clawing at the throats of those who breathed it. Some said the Northside was as much a state of mind as an area, but states of mind don't usually smell that bad.

Hawk and Fisher strolled through the narrow streets, nodding to familiar faces in the bustling crowd. Speed was a way of life in the Northside; there were deals to be made, slights to be avenged, and you never knew who might be coming up behind you. Hawk and Fisher rarely let themselves be hurried. You could miss things that way, and Hawk and Fisher always liked to know what was going on around them. They'd had the Northside as their beat for five years now, on and off, but despite their best efforts, little had changed in that time. For every villain they put away, the Northside produced two more to take his place, and the soul-grinding poverty that was at the root of most crimes never changed from one year to the next. In their most honest moments, Hawk and Fisher knew that all they'd really done was to drive the worst crimes underground, or into other areas. Things tended to be peaceful as long as they were around, but they couldn't be everywhere at once. Occasionally one or the other would talk about quitting, but they never did. They wouldn't give up. It wasn't in their natures. They took each day as it came, and helped those they could. Even little victories were better than none.

The stone-and-timber buildings huddled together as though for warmth, their upper stories leaning out over the streets till their eaves almost touched. Piles of garbage thrust up through the snow and slush, and Hawk and Fisher had to be careful where they put their feet. The garbage collectors came once a month, and then only with an armed guard. The beggars who normally lived off the garbage had been driven from the streets by the cold, but there were still many who braved the bitter weather for their own reasons. Business went on in the Northside, no matter what the weather. Business, and other things.

In the light of a flickering brazier, an angel from the Street of Gods was throwing dice with half a dozen gargoyles. A fast-talking salesman was hawking bracelets plated with something that looked like gold. A large Saint Bernard with a patchy dye job was trying to bum a light for its cigar. Two overlarge rats with human hands were stealing the boots off a dead man. And two nuns were beating up a mugger. Just another day in the Northside.

A sudden burst of pleasant flute music filled Hawk's and Fisher's heads as the Guard communications sorcerer made contact. They stopped to listen and find out what the bad news was. It had to be bad news. It always was. Anything else could have waited till they got back to Headquarters. The flute music broke off abruptly, and was replaced by the dry, acid voice of the communications sorcerer.

Attention all Guards in the North sector. There's a riot in The Crossed Pikes tavern at Salt Lane. There are a large number of dead and injured, including at least two Constables. Approach the situation with extreme caution. There is evidence of chacal use by the rioters.

Hawk and Fisher ran down the street, fighting the snow and slush that dragged at their boots. Salt Lane was four streets away, and a lot could happen in the time it would take them to get there. From the sound of it, too much had happened already. Hawk scowled as he ran. Riots were bad enough without drugs complicating the issue.

Chacal was something new on the streets. Relatively cheap, and easy enough to produce by anyone with a working knowledge of alchemy and access to a bathtub, the drug brought out the animal side of man's nature. It heightened all the senses while turning off the higher functions of the mind, leaving the user little more than a wild animal, free to wallow in the moment and indulge any whim or gratify any desire, free from reason or remorse or any stab of conscience. The drug boosted the users' strength and speed and ferocity, making them almost unstoppable. It also burned out their nervous systems in time, leaving them paralysed or mad or dead from a dozen different causes. But life wasn't worth much in the Northside anyway, and there were all too many who were willing to swap a hopeless future for the savage joys of the present.

Hawk and Fisher charged round the last corner into Salt Lane and then skidded to a halt. A large crowd had already gathered, packing the narrow street from side to side. The two Guards bulled their way through without bothering to be diplomatic about it, and quickly found themselves at the front of the crowd, facing The Crossed Pikes tavern from a safe distance. The tavern looked peaceful enough, apart from its shattered windows, but a Guard Constable was sitting on a nearby doorstep, pressing a bloody handkerchief to a nasty looking scalp wound. Blood covered half his face. He looked up dazedly as Hawk and Fisher approached him, and tried to get to his feet. Hawk waved for him to stay seated.

"What happened here?"

The Constable blinked and licked his dry lips. "My partner and I were first here after the alarm went out. There was fighting and screaming inside the tavern, but we couldn't see anything. The crowd told us there were two Constables already in there, so my partner went in to check things out while I watched the crowd. I waited and waited, but he never came back. After a while it all went quiet, so I decided I'd just take a quick look through the door. I'd barely got my foot over the doorstep when something hit me. I couldn't see for blood in my eyes, so I got out of there quick. I'll try again in a minute, when I've got my breath back. My partner's still in there."

Hawk clapped him on the shoulder reassuringly. "You take a rest. Fisher and I'll have a look. If any more Guards come, keep them out here till we've had a chance to evaluate the situation. Are you sure it's chacal-users in there?"

The Constable shrugged. "That's what the crowd said. But there's no way to be sure. As far as I can tell, anyone who was in the tavern when the trouble started is still in there."

Hawk squeezed the Constable's shoulder comfortingly, and then he and Fisher moved off a way to discuss the matter.

"What do you think?" said Hawk.

"I think we should be very careful how we handle this. I don't like the sound of it at all. Three Guards missing, another injured and so spooked he can't bear to go near the place, and an unknown number of rioters who might just be out of their minds on chacal. The odds stink. How come we never get the easy assignments?"

"There aren't any easy assignments in Haven. We've got to go in, Isobel. There could be innocent people trapped in there, unable to get out."

"It's not very likely, Hawk."

"No, it's not. But we have to check."

Fisher nodded unhappily. "All right; let's do it, before we get a rush of brains to the head and realise what a dumb idea this is. What's the plan?"

"Well, there's no point in trying to sneak in. If there are chacal-users in there, they'll be able to see, hear, and smell us coming long before we even get a glimpse of them. I say we burst in through the door, weapons at the ready, and hit anything that moves."

"Planning never was your strong suit, was it, Hawk?"

"Have you got a better idea?"

"Unfortunately, no."

Hawk grinned. "Then let's do it. Don't look so worried, lass. We've faced worse odds before."

He drew his axe and Fisher drew her sword, and they moved cautiously over to the tavern's main entrance. The door was standing ajar, with only darkness showing beyond. Bright splashes of blood marked the polished wood, below a series of gouges that looked unnervingly like claw marks. Hawk listened carefully, but everything seemed still and quiet. He put his boot against the door and pushed it wide open. The two Captains braced themselves, but nothing happened. Hawk hefted his axe thoughtfully, and glanced at Fisher. She nodded, and they darted through the doorway together. Once inside they moved quickly apart to stand on either side of the door, so they wouldn't be silhouetted against the light, and waited silently for their eyes to adjust to the gloom.

Hawk held his axe out before him, and strained his ears against the silence. A fire was burning fitfully at the far end of the tavern, and some light fell past the shuttered windows. The tavern slowly took form out of the gloom, and Hawk was able to make out chairs and tables overturned and scattered across the floor, as though a sudden storm had swept through the long room, carrying all before it. Dark shapes lay still and silent among the broken furniture, and Hawk didn't need to see them clearly to know they were bodies. He counted fourteen that he was sure of. There was no sign of their killers.

Hawk moved slowly forward, axe at the ready. Broken glass crunched under his boots. Fisher appeared silently out of the gloom to move at his side. He stopped by a wall lamp, and working slowly and carefully, he took out his box of matches and lit it, while Fisher stood guard. It wasn't easy lighting the lamp with one hand, but he wouldn't put his axe down. The sudden light pushed back the darkness, and for the first time Hawk and Fisher were able to see the full extent of the devastation. There was blood everywhere, splashed across the walls and furniture and pooled on the floor. Most of the bodies had been mutilated or disfigured. Some had been torn apart. Loops of purple intestine hung limply from a lamp bracket, and a severed hand beckoned from a barbecue grill by the fire. Most of the bodies had been gutted, ripped open from throat to groin. Whoever or whatever had done it hadn't bothered to use a blade. Fisher swore softly, and her knuckles showed white on her sword hilt. Hawk put the lamp back in its niche, and the two of them moved slowly forward. The tavern was still and silent, full of the stench of blood and death.

They went from body to body, methodically checking for signs of life, but there were none. They found the three Guards who'd gone in to face what they thought was a simple riot. The only way to identify them was by their Constable's scarlet cloak and tunic. Their heads were missing. There was no sign anywhere of their attackers. Hawk wondered briefly if they might have made their escape during the confusion, but he didn't think so. Every instinct he had was screaming at him that the killers were still there, watching, and waiting for their chance. He could almost feel the weight of their gaze on his back.

The tavern's bar had been wrecked. There wasn't an intact bottle or glass left on the shelves, and the floor was covered with a thick carpet of broken glass. Hawk drew Fisher's attention to the bartop. The thick slab of polished mahogany was crisscrossed with long, curving scars that made Hawk think again about claws. He looked at Fisher, who nodded slowly.

"Are you thinking what I'm thinking, Hawk?"

"Could be. We've been working on the assumption this was the work of chacal-users, but more and more this is starting to look like something else entirely. I don't see how anything human could have caused injuries like those, or claw marks like these. I think we've got a werewolf here, Isobel."

Fisher reached down and pulled a silver dagger from inside her boot, and held it loosely in her left hand. Just in case. She moved behind the bar, and then signalled quickly for Hawk to come and join her. He did so, and the two of them stood looking down at the bartender, lying wedged half under the bar. His throat had been torn out, and there were bite marks on his arms where he'd lifted them to defend himself.

"Werewolf," said Fisher.

"Maybe," said Hawk. "I don't know. The bite marks look wrong. A wolf's muzzle would leave a larger, narrower bite. . . ."

Something growled nearby. Hawk and Fisher moved quickly out from behind the bar to give themselves room to fight. They glared about them, but nothing moved in the shadowy, blood-spattered room. The growl came again, louder this time, and then a heavy weight hit Hawk from above and behind, throwing him to the floor. Glass crunched loudly beneath him as he rolled back and forth, trying desperately to tear himself free from the creature that clung to his back, pinning his arms to his sides with its legs and reaching for his throat with clawed hands. He tucked his head in, chin pressed to his chest, and then nearly panicked as he felt teeth gnawing at the back of his head. He got his feet underneath him, glanced quickly about to get his bearings, and then slammed himself back against the heavy wooden bar behind him. The creature's grip loosened as the breath was knocked out of it, and Hawk pulled free. He threw himself to one side, and Fisher stepped forward in a full extended lunge, pinning the creature to the bar with her sword.

For a moment, no one moved. Hawk and Fisher stared incredulously at the blood-soaked man transfixed by Fisher's sword. His clothing hung in rags, and he held his hands like claws. Blood soaked his hands and forearms like crimson gloves, and there was more blood spattered thickly over his livid white flesh. His eyes were wide and staring. He snarled silently at the two Guards, showing his bloody teeth, but he was still just a man. And then he lunged forward, forcing himself along the impaling blade, his bloody hands reaching for Fisher's throat. She held her ground, watching in fascination as the jagged-nailed hands grew steadily nearer. Part of her wondered crazily what had happened to wreck his nails like that.

Hawk lurched to his feet, lifting his axe. The killer lunged forward again, blood spilling down his gut from where Fisher's sword pierced him, snarling and growling like a wild animal. And then Fisher lifted her hand with the silver dagger in it, and cut his throat. Blood sprayed across her arm, and she watched warily as the light went out of his eyes and he slumped forward, dead at last. She pulled out her sword and he fell limply to the floor and lay still. Hawk came over to stand beside her.

"He must have been up in the rafters," he said finally. "All this time, just watching us, and waiting."

Fisher looked up at the ceiling. "There's no one else up there. But I can't believe one man did all this, drug or no drug."

Hawk looked down at the dead user. "Maybe we shouldn't have killed him after all. There are a lot of questions we could have asked him."

"He didn't exactly give us a choice," said Fisher dryly. "Besides, he wouldn't have been allowed to talk. We'd have had to keep him in gaol till he came down, and by then word would have reached his suppliers. They'd either have sprung him or killed him to keep his mouth shut."

Hawk scowled. "It has to be said Headquarters' security isn't worth spit these days. Particularly when it comes to drug arrests. You know, it wasn't this bad when we first joined the Guard."

"Yes it was," said Fisher. "We just weren't experienced enough to recognise the signs. There's a lot of money in drugs, and where there's a lot of money there's a line of Guards with their hands out."

"This day started out depressing," said Hawk, "and it's not getting any better. Let's get the hell out of here and file our report. If one chacal-user can do this much damage on a rampage, then this city is in for some interesting times."

A low growl trembled on the air behind them. Hawk and Fisher spun round, weapons at the ready. The tavern looked just as still and quiet as before. None of the bodies had moved. The growl came again, but this time low and subdued, sounding almost more like a groan. Hawk glared in the direction of the sound, and his gaze came to rest on an overturned table leaning against a wall. It was a big table, with room for one, maybe two, people behind it. Hawk silently indicated the table to Fisher, and they moved slowly forward. There were no more growls or groans, but as he drew nearer, Hawk thought he could hear something dripping. Something . . . feeding.

They reached the table in a matter of moments, moving silently through the gloom. Hawk put away his axe and grabbed the rim of the table with both hands, while Fisher stood ready with her sword. They counted to three silently together, and then Hawk braced himself and pulled the heavy table away from the wall with one swift movement. Fisher moved quickly forward to stand between him and whatever was waiting, and then both she and Hawk stood very still as the table revealed its secret.

The second chacal-user was a young woman, maybe seventeen or eighteen. Her face was bone-white, with dark, staring eyes, and her hands and forearms were slick with other people's blood. She held her hands like claws, but made no move to attack Hawk or Fisher. Someone, presumably the other user, had ripped open her stomach. It was a wide, hideous wound that should have killed her immediately, but the chacal was keeping her alive. She lay propped against the wall in a widening pool of her own blood, and as Hawk and Fisher watched she dipped a hand into the ragged wound in her gut, pulled out a bloody morsel, and ate it.

Oh, dear God, she's been feeding on herself. . . .

Hawk moved forward, and put a gentle restraining hand on the girl's arm. "Don't. Please don't."

"Get away from her, Hawk. She's still dangerous. We don't know how many people she's killed here."

"Get a doctor," said Hawk, without looking round.

"Hawk . . ."

"Get a doctor!"

Fisher nodded, and hurried over to the main door. Hawk put the girl's hand in her lap, and brushed her long, stringy hair from her face. The user looked at him for the first time.

"Something went wrong," she said slowly, her voice barely rising above a murmur. Hawk had to lean close to understand her. Her breath smelled of blood and something worse. Her dead white skin was beaded with sweat. "This wasn't supposed to happen. They said it would make us feel like Gods. I'm cold."

"I've sent for a doctor," said Hawk. "Take it easy. Save your strength."

"They lied to us. . . ."

"Can you tell me what happened?" said Hawk. "You said something went wrong. What went wrong?"

"It was a new drug. Supposed to be the best. Like chacal, only stronger. We were going to be like Gods. We were packing it up at the factory, ready to ship it out. Leon took some, for a lark. We tried it here, just a little. And then everything went bad."

"Tell me about the factory," said Hawk. "Where is it?"

The girl's hand drifted towards her wound again. Hawk stopped it, and put it back in her lap. She looked at him. "I'm cold."

Hawk took off his cloak and wrapped it around her. She was shivering violently, and sweat ran down her face in rivulets. There was no color left in her face. Even her lips were white. Her breathing grew increasingly shallow, and when she spoke Hawk had to concentrate hard to make out the words.

"Morgan's place. The Blue Dolphin. In the Hook."

"All right, lass, take it easy. That's all I need. We'll get the bastards. You rest now. The doctor will be here soon."

"Would you hold my hand? Please?"

"Sure." Hawk took off one of his gloves and held her left hand, squeezing it comfortingly. Warm blood spilled down his wrist. "All right?"

"Hold it up where I can see it. I can't feel it."

Hawk started to lift her hand up before her face, but she'd stopped breathing. He was still holding her hand when Fisher finally came back with the Guard doctor.

"I didn't even find out her name," said Hawk, pulling his cloak around his shoulders. Guard Constables and Captains summoned to the scene by the communications sorcerer spilled around Hawk and Fisher as they moved in and out of The Crossed Pikes tavern. They were carrying out the dead and lining them up in neat rows on the snow, ready for the meat wagon when it arrived. The Guard doctor hovered over them like an anxious relative, making notes on cause of death, for when the forensic sorcerer arrived. A large crowd had gathered, but were being kept back by two Constables. Hawk knelt down suddenly, and started roughly cleaning the blood from his hand with a handful of snow. Fisher put a hand on his shoulder and squeezed it comfortingly.

"You did all you could, Hawk."

"I know that."

"She killed at least a dozen people in there. Probably more."

"I know that too." He got to his feet and pulled his glove back on. "Before she died, she told me where they're making the stuff she took. It's Robbie Morgan's place, down in the Devil's Hook."

Fisher looked at him sharply. "Standard procedure would be to contact Headquarters and tell them the factory's location. Since you haven't done that, I assume there's a good reason why not?"

"I want these bastards, Isobel. I want them bad. It's a new drug, you see; they haven't released it yet. Can you imagine what the Northside will be like once this super-chacal hits the streets? We've got to stop it now. While we can."

"So let the Drug Squad handle it. That's what they're paid for."

"Oh no; I'm not risking this one going wrong. You can guarantee some Guard would tip Morgan off, in return for a sweetener. The Drug Squad would get there just a little too late and find nothing but an empty warehouse. That's happened too many times just recently. So I think we'll do this one ourselves."

"Us? You mean, just you and me?"

"Isobel, please; I haven't gone completely crazy. Morgan's probably got a small army of security people protecting the Blue Dolphin. But we've got a small army ourselves, right here. There's a dozen Constables, five Captains, and even a sorceress. We'll leave a few people here to mind the store, and take the rest."

"On whose authority?"

"Mine. If we bring this off, no one's going to ask any questions."

"And if we don't?"

Hawk looked at her steadily. "This is important to me, Isobel. She died right in front of me, scared and hurting, and there wasn't a damn thing I could do to help her. Just this once, we've got a chance to make a difference. A real difference. Let's do it."

"All right. Let's do it. But how are we going to get the others to go along on an unofficial raid?"

Hawk smiled. "Easy. We won't tell them it's unofficial."

Fisher grinned back at him. "I like the way you think, Hawk."

They finally ended up with an impromptu task force of ten Constables, two more Captains, and the sorceress Mistique; all blithely unaware that they were about to break every rule in the book. Which was probably for the best. That way, if anything did go wrong, Hawk and Fisher could take all the blame on themselves. Besides, no one with the brains they were born with would have volunteered if they'd known the truth. At which point Hawk decided very firmly that he wasn't going to think about the situation anymore. It was depressing him too much. All that mattered was shutting down the drug factory, and Morgan as well, if possible.

Hawk had heard about Morgan. Most people in Haven had, one way or another. He'd made enough money down the years from drugs, prostitution, and murder to buy himself respectability. He was seen in all the best places, belonged to all the right clubs, and these days was officially regarded as above suspicion. In fact, he still had a dirty finger in every pie in Haven, though no one had ever been able to prove anything. But Hawk and Fisher knew, like every other Guard. They had to deal every day with the violence and suffering his businesses caused. Hawk frowned thoughtfully. It wasn't like Morgan to get so personally involved in a scheme like this, having the super-chacal packed and distributed from one of his own warehouses. And it also wasn't like him to get involved with such a dangerous drug. The more traditional drugs brought less publicity, were just as addictive, and therefore just as profitable. Hawk shrugged mentally. Every villain makes a mistake sooner or later, and Morgan had made a bad one.

Hawk and Fisher led their people through the Northside at a quick march, heading for the Devil's Hook. They made an impressive spectacle, and the crowds drew back to let them pass. It was almost like a parade, but nobody cheered. The law wasn't popular in the Northside. Hawk looked back at his people, and smiled to himself. They might just bring this off after all. The Constables were some of the toughest Guards in Haven. They had to be, or they wouldn't have been working the Northside. And he knew both the Captains, by reputation, if not personally.

Captain Andrew Doughty was a medium-height, stocky man in his late forties; a career Guard, with all the courage, cunning, and native caution that implied. He was blond-haired, blue-eyed, and glacially handsome, and his job was his life. He had a good enough reputation with his sword that he didn't have to keep proving it, but he liked to anyway, given the chance. He'd had a lot of partners in his time, but worked best alone. Mostly because he didn't trust anyone but himself.

Captain Howard Burns was a tall, lean man in his late thirties, with an unruly mop of dark hair and a thick spade beard. He was an expert in personal and company security, and worked mostly in the Westside, overseeing the transfer of money or valuables from one location to another. He took his work very seriously, and had several official commendations for bravery. He had no sense of humour at all, but then, no one's perfect. Especially not in Haven.

Hawk had worked with both of them in his time, and was glad he had someone apart from Fisher to watch his back this time. They were both good men, men he could depend on. The only real wild card in the pack was the sorceress Mistique. She was new to the Guard, and still looking for a chance to show what she could do. Mistique was a tall, slender, fluttering woman in her early thirties, dressed in sorcerer's black, carefully cut in the latest fashion to show lots of bare flesh. If the cold bothered her at all, she didn't show it. She had a long, horsey face, and a friendly, toothy grin that made her look ten years younger. She had a husky, upper-class accent and wouldn't answer questions about her background. She also had a thick mass of long black curly hair she had to keep sweeping back out of her eyes. All together, she wasn't exactly the most organized person Hawk had ever met, but she was supposed to be bloody good at what she did, and he'd settle for that. Morgan's warehouse would undoubtedly be crawling with defensive magic and booby traps. The only real problem with Mistique was that she hardly ever seemed to stop talking. And she wore literally dozens of beads and bangles and bracelets that clattered loudly as she walked. Hawk made a mental note not to include her in any plans that involved sneaking up on the enemy.

And then they came to the Devil's Hook, and Mistique's chatter stumbled to a halt. Even casual conversation died away quickly as Hawk led his people into the Hook. It was a bad place to be, and they all knew it. The Devil's Hook was the single poorest, most decayed, and most dangerous area in Haven. A square mile of slums and alleyways backing onto the main Docks, the Hook held more crime, corruption, and open misery than most people could bear to think about. The squalid tenement buildings were crammed with sweatshops that paid starvation wages for work on goods that often fetched high prices in the better parts of the city. Child labour was common, as was malnutrition and disease. No one ventured into the stinking streets alone or unarmed. The Guard patrolled the Hook very loosely rather than risk open warfare with the gangs who ran it. The gangs weren't as powerful as they once were, thanks to some sterling work by the sorcerer Gaunt, but after he left Haven the bad times soon returned as new gangs established themselves and fought for territory. Nobody was surprised. No one made any complaints. The Hook was where you ended up when you had nowhere else to go but a pauper's grave.

All in all, the perfect spot for a new drug factory.

The Blue Dolphin was a squalid little lock-up warehouse, on one end of a rotting tenement. Chemicals from nearby factories had stained and pitted the stonework, and all the windows were boarded up. It was cheaper than shutters. The street was deserted, but Hawk could feel the pressure of watching eyes. He brought his people to a halt outside the warehouse, and quickly set up a defensive perimeter. The last thing they needed was a gang attack while they were occupied with the drug factory. Fisher moved in close beside him.

"Are you sure this is the right place, Hawk? If Morgan's got a packing and distribution setup here, he's going to need a lot more room than this pokey little warehouse."

"This is the place," said Hawk, hoping he sounded more convinced than he felt. When all was said and done, all he had to go on was the dying words of a girl already out of her mind on chacal. He pushed the thought to one side. He'd believed her then; he had to believe her now. Or she had died for nothing.

"There are mystic wards all over the place," said Mistique. Hawk jumped slightly. He hadn't heard her come up behind him. The sorceress smiled briefly, and then turned her attention back to the warehouse. "I can't quite make out what kind of wards, though. Given the circumstances, I think we ought to tread carefully, just in case."

Hawk nodded, and gestured to two of the Constables. They moved forward and cautiously tried the warehouse door. It was locked, which surprised no one. One Constable kicked the door. His clothes burst into flames that leapt up around him in seconds. He screamed shrilly and staggered back, beating at his blazing clothes with his hands. The other Constable quickly pulled him down and rolled him back and forth in the snow to smother the flames. Hawk scowled. He hadn't expected to hit a magic defence this quickly. He made sure the injured Constable would be all right, and then turned to the sorceress.

"Get us in there, Mistique. I don't care how you do it, but do it fast. They know we're here now."

The sorceress nodded eagerly, her earrings jangling accompaniment. She stared thoughtfully at the door, and wisps of fog began to appear around her, circling and twisting on the still air. The misty grey strands grew thicker, undulating disturbingly as they drifted away from the sorceress towards the warehouse door. The mists looked almost alive, and purposeful. They curled around the door, seeping past the edges and sinking into the wood itself. Mistique made a sudden, sharp gesture and the door exploded. Fragments and splinters of rotting wood rained down on the Guards as they shielded themselves with their cloaks. Where the door had been, there was now nothing but an impenetrable darkness.

Mistique turned to look at Hawk. Strands of fog still swirled around her, like ethereal serpents with no beginning or end. "Fast enough for you, darling?"

"Very impressive," said Hawk courteously, trying hard not to sound too impressed. "Can you tell us anything about what's beyond the doorway?"

"That's the bad news, I'm afraid," said Mistique. "The darkness is a dimensional gateway, leading to a small pocket dimension, the inside of which is a damn sight bigger than that lock-up. I've knocked out the protective wards so we can get in there, but I've absolutely no idea of what might be waiting for us. Sorry to be such a drag, but whoever designed this beastly setup was jolly good at his job."

"All right," said Hawk. "We'll just have to take it as it comes. Brace yourselves, people; we're going in. I want Morgan alive, and preferably intact so we can ask him questions. Anyone else is fair game. I'd prefer prisoners to corpses, but don't put yourselves at risk. We don't know what kind of odds we'll be facing. Try not to wreck the place too much; you never know what might turn out to be useful evidence. Right. Let's do it."

He hefted his axe and walked forward, Fisher and Mistique on either side of him. From behind came a brief whisper of steel on leather as the Guards drew their weapons and started after him. Hawk gritted his teeth and plunged into the darkness. There was a sharp moment of intense heat, and then he burst through into Morgan's factory. His first sight of the place was almost enough to stop him in his tracks, but he forced himself to keep going to make room for the others coming behind. Morgan's warehouse was an insane mixture of planes and angles and inverted stairways that could not have existed in anything but a pocket universe.

There was no up or down, in any way that made any sense. People walked on one side of a surface or another, or on both, and gravity seemed merely a matter of opinion. Simple wooden stairways connected the various level planes, twisting and turning around each other like mating snakes, and walls became floors became ceilings, depending on which way you approached them. Hawk shook off his disorientation and concentrated on the force of armed men rushing towards him from a dozen different directions.

He didn't have to count them to know his own small group was vastly outnumbered.

"Mistique!" he yelled quickly. "Take out the stairways. Bring this place down around their ears!"

"I'm afraid we have a slight problem, dear," said the sorcerer, staring off into the distance. "Morgan has his own sorceress here, and I'm rather tied up at the moment keeping him from killing us all."

"Can you take him?"

"Probably, if you stop interrupting. And if you can keep those nasty-looking men-at-arms away from me."

Hawk yelled instructions to his people, and the Constables moved forward to form a barrier between Mistique and the approaching men-at-arms, while Captain Doughty and Captain Burns stayed at her side as bodyguards. Fisher looked at Hawk.

"And what are we going to do?"

"Find Morgan," said Hawk grimly. "I'm not taking any chances on his getting away. Mistique, when you're ready, don't wait for orders from me. Just trash the place."

Mistique nodded, absorbed in her sorcerous battle. Thick strands of fog twisted around her like dogs straining at the leash. Hawk started down the nearest stairway, with Fisher close behind him. They hadn't gone far when Hawk heard the first clash of steel as his people met the men-at-arms. He didn't look back.

In what might have been the centre of the mad tangle of planes and stairways was a more-or-less open area with a lot of excited movement. It seemed as good a place as any to start looking. The stairs turned and twisted under Hawk, and he quickly learned to keep his gaze on his feet and ignore what was going on around him. A man-at-arms in full chain mail came running up the stairs, waving his sword with more confidence than style. Hawk cut him down with a single blow, and hurled his body over the side of the stairway. The dead man fell in half a dozen different directions before disappearing from sight in the maze of stairways.

More men-at-arms came charging towards Hawk, six

men in the lead, with a lot more on the way. Bad odds, on a rickety wooden staircase. He looked quickly about him, and grinned as he spotted a large flat plane not too far away. It stood at right angles to him, but then, so did the two men on it, frantically packing paper parcels into two large crates on a wide table. He looked back at Fisher, and pointed at the plane. She raised an eyebrow, and then nodded sharply. They clambered up onto the narrow wooden banister, which creaked dangerously under their weight, and leapt out into space towards the right-angled plane. Gravity changed suddenly as they left the stairs, and slammed them down hard on the bare wooden plane.

Hawk and Fisher hit the floor rolling, and were quickly up on their feet again. The two men packing were already gone. Hawk hefted one of the small paper parcels, and then looked at the size of the packing case. That crate could hold an awful lot of drugs . . . if it was drugs. A horrible thought struck him, and he opened the packet and sniffed cautiously at the grey powder inside. He relaxed slightly and blew his nose hard. It was chacal. The sharp acidic smell was quite distinctive. Fisher yelled a warning, and he threw the packet aside and looked up. A man-at-arms leaned out from an upside-down stairway overhead and cut at Hawk with his sword. Hawk parried with his axe, but couldn't reach high enough to attack the man. He backed away, and the swordsman moved along the stairway after him. There was a strange, dreamlike quality to the fight, with both men upside-down to the other, but Hawk knew better than to let the strangeness distract him. If he couldn't figure out a way to get at his opponent, he was a dead man. An axe wasn't made for defence. He bumped into the table, and an idea struck him. He grabbed the open packet and threw the chacal powder into the other man's face. The man-at-arms screamed, and dropped his sword to claw at his eyes with both hands.

"Hawk!"

He spun round to find Fisher standing at the edge of the plane, fighting off three of the five men-at-arms who'd jumped down off the banister after the Guards. Two already lay dead at her feet. Hawk sprinted over to join her, ducked under the first man's sword, and swung his axe in a vicious sideways arc. The heavy steel axehead punched through the man's chain mail and buried itself in his rib cage. Bones broke and splintered, and the impact drove the man-at-arms to his knees, coughing blood. Hawk yanked the axe free and booted the man off the edge of the plane. The dying man fell upwards out of sight.

Fisher had already cut down another of her opponents, and now stood toe to toe with the last remaining adversary. Steel rang on steel and sparks flew as the blades met, hammering together and dancing apart in a lightning duel of strength and skill. Hawk started forward to help her, and then stopped as he saw more men-at-arms running down a winding stairway to join the fight. Fisher saw them too, and quickly kneed her opponent in the groin.

"Get the hell out of here, Hawk. Find Morgan. I'll hold them off." She cut her opponent's throat, and sidestepped neatly to avoid the jetting blood. "Move it, Hawk!"

Hawk nodded abruptly, and turned and ran down the other stairway, heading once again for what had looked like the centre of operations. From behind him came the clash of sword on sword as Fisher met the first of the new onslaught, but he didn't look back. He didn't dare. He pressed on through the maze, passing from stairway to plane to stairway and cutting down anyone who tried to get in his way. All around him Morgan's people were running back and forth, looking for orders or weapons or just heading for the exit. Morgan wouldn't have gone, though. This was his place, his territory, and he'd trust in his men and his sorcerer to protect him. A sudden piercing scream caught Hawk's attention, and he looked up and round in time to see a man dressed in sorcerer's black stagger drunkenly across a plane at right angles to Hawk's stairway. Streamers of thick milky fog burst out of his mouth and eyes and ears. His head swelled impossibly and then exploded in a spreading cloud of crimson mist. The body crumpled to the floor as the last echo of the sorcerer's dying cry faded slowly away.

Hawk grinned. So much for Morgan's sorcerer. He was

close to the centre now; he could feel it. There were drugs and people and men-at-arms everywhere, and there, straight ahead, he saw a familiar face in an earth-brown cloak and hood. Morgan. Hawk ran forward, cutting his way through two swordsmen foolish enough to try and stop him. Their blood splashed across his face and hands, but he didn't pause to wipe it off. He couldn't let Morgan escape. He couldn't.

Hold my hand. Hold it up where I can see it. . . .

Morgan looked once at the bloodstained Guard rushing towards him, and then continued stuffing papers into a leather pouch. Three men-at-arms moved forward to stand between Hawk and Morgan. Hawk hit them at a dead run, swinging his axe double-handed. He never felt the wounds he took, and when it was all over, he stepped across their dead bodies to advance slowly on the drug baron.

Seen up close, Morgan didn't look like much. Average height and build, with a bland face, perhaps a little too full to be handsome. A mild gaze and a civilised smile. He didn't look like the kind of man who'd made his fortune through the death and suffering of others. But then, they never did. Hawk moved slowly forward. Blood ran thickly down from a wound in his left thigh, and squelched inside his boot. There was more blood, soaking his arms and sides, some of it his. Even so, Morgan had enough sense not to try and run. He knew he wouldn't make it. They stood facing each other, while from all around came shouts and screams and the sounds of fighting.

"Who are you?" said Morgan finally. "Why are you doing this?"

"I'm every bad dream you ever had," said Hawk. "I'm a Guard who can't be bought."

Morgan shook his head slowly, as a father chides a son who has made an understandable mistake. "Everyone has his price, Captain. If not you, then certainly someone among your superiors. I'll never come to trial. I know too much, about too many people. And I really do have friends in high places. Quite often, I helped put them there. So I'm afraid all this blood and destruction has been for nothing.

You won't be able to make a case against me."

Hawk grinned. "You're the second person who's told me that today. He was wrong, too. You're going to hang, Morgan. I'll come and watch."

There was a muffled sound from behind a drapery to their right. Morgan glanced at it, and then looked quickly away. For the first time, he seemed a little uneasy. Hawk moved slowly over to the curtain, unconsciously favouring his wounded leg.

"What's behind here, Morgan?"

"Experimental animals. We had to test the drug, to establish the correct dosage. Nothing that would interest you."

Hawk swept the cloth to one side, and froze for a moment. Inside a crude, steel-barred cage lay a pile of dead young men and women, tangled together. Some were barely teenagers. The bodies were torn and mutilated, and it was clear most of them had died tearing at each other and themselves. One man's hand was buried to the wrist in another's ripped-open stomach. A young girl had torn out her own eyes. There was blood everywhere, but not enough to hide the characteristic colorless white skin of chacal use. Hawk turned back to Morgan, who hadn't moved an inch.

"Where did you get them?" said Hawk.

Morgan shrugged. "Runaways, debtors' prisons, even a few volunteers. There are always some ready to risk their lives for a new thrill."

"You know what this new drug does," said Hawk. "So why are you getting involved with it? There isn't enough bribe money in the world to make the Guard overlook the slaughter this shit will cause. Even the other drug barons would turn against you over something like this."

"I won't be here when it breaks," said Morgan. "There's a lot of money in this. Millions of ducats. More than enough to leave Haven and set up a new and very comfortable life somewhere else. You could have a life like that, Captain. There's enough money for everyone. Just name your price, and I guarantee you I can meet it."

"Really?" said Hawk. He stepped forward suddenly, grabbed a handful of Morgan's robe and dragged him over to the steel cage. "You want to know my price, Morgan? Bring them back to life. Bring those poor bastards back! Go on; give just one of them his life back and I'll let you go, here and now."

"You're being ridiculous, Captain," said Morgan evenly. "And very foolish."

"You're under arrest," said Hawk. "Tell your people to lay down their weapons and surrender."

"Or?"

Hawk grinned. "Believe me, Morgan, you don't want to know."

"I'll have to speak to my sorcerer first."

"Don't bother; he's dead."

Morgan looked at him blankly, and then open terror rushed across his face. "We've got to get out of here! If he's dead, this whole place could collapse at any moment. It's only his magic that kept it stable!"

Hawk swore briefly. He knew real fear when he saw it. "Tell your men to surrender. Do it!"

Morgan started shouting orders, and all over the maze of planes and stairways the fighting came to a halt. Hawk yelled orders to his men, and the Guards began herding Morgan's people towards the dimensional portal. Hawk dragged Morgan along himself, never once releasing his grip on the drug baron's robe. The stairway began to sway and tremble under his feet. A nearby plane cracked across from end to end. Streams of dust fell from somewhere high above. There were creaks and groanings all around, and the wooden handrail turned to rot and mush under Hawk's hand. Morgan began pleading with him to go faster. Mistique appeared out of nowhere in a clattering of beads and bracelets and ran beside them as they hurried towards the portal.

"So, you did get the little rat after all. Well done, darling."

"I wish you wouldn't call me that in front of the men," said Hawk. "Can you use your magic to hold this place together long enough for us all to get out?"

"I'm doing my best, darling, but it's not really my field.

We should all make it. If we're lucky."

They reached the portal to find it bottlenecked by the last of Morgan's people. The drug baron screamed at them to get out of the way, but Hawk held him back. Guards encouraged the slow movers on their way with harsh language and the occasional kick up the backside. The remaining stairways broke apart and collapsed in a roar of cracking timber. The planes spun and twisted in midair, fraying at the edges. Loose magic snapped on the air like disturbed static. The last of Morgan's people went through, and Hawk and Morgan and Mistique followed the Guards out.

The cold of the street hit Hawk like a blow, and his vision clouded briefly as pain and fatigue caught up with him. He shook his head and pushed the tiredness back. He didn't have time for it now. He handed Morgan over to two Constables, along with dire threats of what he'd do to them if Morgan escaped, and looked round for familiar faces. Fisher appeared out of nowhere, safe and more or less sound. They compared wounds for a moment, and then hugged each other carefully. Captain Burns came over to join them as they broke apart. He looked bloodied and battered and just a little dazed.

"How many did we lose?" said Hawk.

Burns scowled. "Five Constables, and Captain Doughty. Could have been worse, I suppose. Though I won't tell Doughty's widow that. Did you get Morgan?"

"Yeah," said Fisher. "Hawk got him."

And then there was a great crashing roar, and the whole tenement behind them collapsed amid screams of rending stone and timber, and the death cries of the hundreds of people trapped within. Flying fragments of stone and wood tore through the air like shrapnel, and then a thick cloud of smoke billowed out to fill the street from end to end.

2

Going Down

Hawk pulled and tugged at a stubborn piece of rubble, and bit by bit it slid aside. The stone's sharp edges tore at his gloves and the flesh beneath, but he hardly felt the pain through the bitter cold and the creeping numbness of utter exhaustion. He'd lost track of how long he and the others had been digging through the wreckage, searching for survivors. It seemed ages since the collapsing pocket dimension had pulled the whole tenement building down with it, but the air was still thick with dust that choked the throat and irritated the eye. There were still occasional screams or moans or pleas for help from people trapped deep within the huge pile of broken stone and timber, which stretched across the narrow street and lapped up against the opposite building.

Hawk supposed he should be grateful that only the one building had come down, but he was too numb to feel much of anything now. He looked slowly about him as he stopped for a brief rest. The adjoining buildings were slumped and stooped, with jagged cracks in their walls, yet somehow holding together. The Guard had evacuated them, just in case, and their occupants had willingly joined the dig for survivors. Even in the Devil's Hook, people could sometimes be touched by tragedy.

There was no telling how many might still be trapped under the debris. Slum landlords didn't keep records on how many desperate people they squeezed into each dingy little room. The Guard were trying to keep a count, but most of the dead they dug out were too disfigured to be easily identified, and sometimes all that could be found of the bodies were scattered bits and pieces. The rescuers worked on, fired now and then from their exhaustion by the sudden appearance of a living soul, pulled raw and bloodied from the darkness under the rubble. Guards and prisoners worked side by side, along with people from the Hook, all animosities forgotten in the driving need to save as many as they could.

Not that everyone had proved so openhearted. Morgan had flatly refused to lift so much as a finger to help. Hawk was already half out of his mind with concern for the injured, and knew he couldn't spare even one Constable to watch over the drug baron. So he just punched Morgan out, manacled the unconscious man to a nearby railing and left him there. No one objected, not even his own people. A few of them even cheered. Hawk smiled briefly at the memory, and returned to work.

They had no real tools to work with, so they attacked the broken bricks and stone and wood with their bare hands, forming human chains to transfer the larger pieces. They worked with frantic speed, spurred on by the screams and sobbing of those trapped below, but soon found it was better to work slowly and carefully rather than risk the debris collapsing in on itself, if a vital support was unwittingly removed. Most of the bodies were women and children, crushed and broken by the horrid weight. Crammed together in one room sweatshops and factories, they never stood a chance. But some survived, sheltered by protecting slabs of masonry, and they were reason enough to keep on digging.

And all the time he worked, Hawk was haunted by a simple, inescapable thought; it was all his fault. If he hadn't led the raid on Morgan's factory, the pocket dimension wouldn't have collapsed, taking the tenement with it, and all those people, all those women and children, would still be alive.

Eventually the fire brigade arrived, encouraged by the presence of so many Guards. Normally they wouldn't have entered the Devil's Hook without an armed escort and a written guarantee of hazard pay. They quickly took over the running of the operation, and things began to go more smoothly. They set about propping up the adjoining buildings, and dealt efficiently with the many water leaks. Doctors and nurses arrived from a nearby charity hospital, and began sorting out the real emergencies from the merely badly injured. Fisher took the opportunity to drag Hawk over to a doctor, and insisted he have his wounds treated. He didn't have the strength to argue.

More volunteers turned up to help, followed by a small army of looters. Hawk waited for the doctor to finish the healing spell, and then rose to his feet, feeling stiff but a damn sight more lively. He walked over to confront the looters, Fisher at his side. The first few took one look at what was coming towards them, went very pale, and skidded to a halt. Word passed quickly back, and most of the would-be looters decided immediately that they were needed somewhere else, very urgently. The ones who couldn't move or think that fast found themselves volunteered to help dig through the rubble for survivors.

The work continued, interrupted increasingly rarely by a sudden shout as someone thought they heard a cry for help. Everyone would stop where they were, ears straining against the quiet as they tried to locate the faint sound. Sometimes there was nothing but the quiet, and work would slowly resume, but sometimes the cry would come again, and then everyone would work together, sweating and straining against the stubborn stone and wood until the survivors could be gently lifted free. There were hundreds of dead in the rubble, and only a few dozen living, but each new life snatched from the crushing stone gave the exhausted volunteers new will to carry on. Nurses moved among the workers with cups of hot soup and mulled ale, and an encouraging word for those who looked as though they needed it. And still more volunteers came to help, drawn from the surrounding area by the scale of the tragedy.

More Guards arrived, expecting riots, chaos, and mass looting, and were shocked to find so many people from the Hook working together to help others. Fisher set some of them to blocking off the street, to keep out sightseers and ghouls who'd just get in the way, and put the rest to work digging in the ruins, so that those who'd been working the longest could get some rest. Some of the Guard Constables weren't too keen on dirtying their hands with manual labour, but one cold glare from Hawk was enough to convince them to shut up and get on with it.

It was at this point that the local gang leader, Hammer, arrived, along with twenty or so of his most impressive-looking bullies, and insisted on talking to the man in charge. Hawk went over to meet him, secretly glad of an excuse for a break—and a little guilty at feeling that way. So he wasn't in the best of moods when the gang leader delivered his ultimatum. Hammer was a medium-height, well-padded man in his early twenties. He dressed well, if rather flashily, and had the kind of face that fell naturally into a sneer.

"What the hell do you think you're doing here?" he said flatly. "This is my territory, and no one works here without paying me. No one. So either pay up, right here, where everyone can see it, or I'll be forced to order my people to shut you down. Nothing happens in my territory without my permission."

Hawk looked at him. "There are injured people here who need our help. Some of them will die without it."

"That's your problem."

Hawk nodded, and kneed Hammer in the groin. All the color went out of the gang leader's face, and he dropped to his knees, his hands buried between his thighs.

"You're under arrest," said Hawk. He looked hard at the shocked bullies. "The rest of you, get over there and start digging, or I'll personally cut you all off at the knees."

The bullies looked at him, looked at their fallen leader, and decided he just might mean it. They shrugged more or less in unison, and moved over to work in the ruins. The

local people raised a brief cheer for Hawk, surprising him
and them, and then they all got back to work. The gang
leader was left lying huddled in a ball, handcuffed by his
ankle to a railing.

The hours dragged on, and the search turned up fewer
and fewer survivors. The fire brigade's engineers set up
supports for the adjoining buildings; nothing elaborate, but
enough to keep them secure until the builders could be
called in. People began to drift away, too exhausted or
dispirited to continue. Hawk sent most of his Guards back
to Headquarters with Morgan and his people, the crates of
chacal now carefully labelled and numbered, and the gang
leader Hammer, under Captain Burns's direction. But Hawk
stayed on, and Fisher stayed with him. Hawk didn't know
whether he stayed because he felt he was still needed or
because he was punishing himself, but he knew he couldn't
leave until he was sure there was no one still alive under the
wreckage. Someone cried out they'd heard something, and
once again everything came to a halt as the diggers listened,
holding their breath, trying to hear a faint cry for help over
the beating of their own hearts. One of the men yelled, and
everyone converged on a dark, narrow shaft that fell away
into the depths of the ruins. One of the diggers dropped a
small stone down the shaft. They all listened hard, but no
one heard it hit bottom.

"Sounded like a child," said the man who first raised the
alarm. "Pretty quiet. Must be trapped at the bottom of the
shaft somewhere."

"We daren't try to widen the hole," said Fisher. "This
whole area is touchy as hell. One wrong move, and the
shaft could collapse in on itself."

"We can't just leave the child there," said a woman dully,
kneeling at the edge of the shaft. "Someone could go down
on a rope, and fetch it up."

"Not someone," said Hawk. "Me. Get me a length of rope
and a lantern."

He started stripping off his cloak and furs. Fisher moved
in close beside him. "You don't have to do this, Hawk."

"Yes I do."

"You couldn't have known this would happen."

"I should have thought, instead of just barging straight in."

"That shaft isn't stable. It could collapse at any time."

"I know that. Keep an eye on my furs and my axe, would you? This is Haven, after all."

He stood by the shaft in his shirt and trousers, looking down into the darkness, and shivered suddenly, not entirely from the cold. He didn't like dark, enclosed places, particularly underground, and the whole situation reminded him uncomfortably of a bad experience he'd once had down a mine. He didn't have to go down the shaft. There were any number of others ready to volunteer. But if he didn't do it, he'd always believe he should have.

Someone came back with a length of rope, and Fisher fastened one end round his waist. Someone else tied the other end to a sturdy outcropping of broken stone, and Hawk and Fisher took turns tugging on the rope to make sure it was secure. One of the men gave him a lantern, and he held it out over the shaft. The pale golden light didn't penetrate far into the darkness. He listened, but couldn't hear anything. The hole itself was about three feet in diameter and looked distinctly unsafe. Hawk shrugged. It wouldn't get any safer, no matter how long he waited. He sat down on the edge, very slowly and very carefully, swung his legs over the side, and then lowered himself into the darkness, bracing his back and his knees against the sides of the shaft. He took a deep breath and let it out, and then inch by inch he made his way down into the darkness, the lantern resting uncomfortably on his chest.

Jagged edges of stone and wood cut at him viciously as he descended, and the circle of daylight overhead grew smaller and smaller. He moved slowly down in his pool of light, stopping now and again to call out to the child below, but there was never any reply. He pressed on, cursing the narrow confines around him as they bowed in and out, and soon came to the bottom of the shaft. He held up the lantern and looked around him. Rough spikes of broken wood and stone protruded from every side, and a dozen openings led

off into the honeycomb of wreckage. Most were too small
or too obviously unsafe for him to try, but one aperture led
into a narrow tunnel barely two feet high. Hawk called out
to the child, but there was only the silence and his own
harsh breathing. He looked back up the main shaft, but all
he could see was darkness. He was on his own. He looked
again at the narrow tunnel, cursed again briefly, and got
down on his hands and knees.

The rope played out behind him as he wriggled his way
through the tunnel darkness in his narrow pool of light,
stopping now and then to manoeuvre past outcroppings
from the tunnel walls. The child had to be around here
somewhere. He couldn't have come all this way for nothing. He thought briefly about the sheer weight of wreckage
pressing from above, and his skin went cold. The roof of
the tunnel bulged down ahead of him, and he had to lie
on his back and force himself past the obstruction an inch
at a time, pulling the lantern behind. The unyielding stone
pressed against his chest like a giant hand trying to crush
the breath out of him. He breathed out, emptying his lungs,
and slowly squeezed past.

In the end, he found the child by bumping into her. He'd
just got past the obstruction when his head hit something
soft and yielding. His first thought was that he'd run into
some kind of animal down in the dark with him, and his
imagination conjured up all kinds of unpleasantness before
he got it back under control. He squirmed over onto his
stomach, wishing briefly that he'd brought his axe, and then
stopped as he saw her, lying still and silent on the tunnel
floor. She looked to be about five or six years old, covered
in dirt and blood, but still breathing strongly. Hawk spoke
to her, but she didn't respond, even when he tapped her
sharply on the shoulder. He pulled himself along beside her,
and saw for the first time that one of her legs was pinned
between two great slabs of stone, holding her firmly just
below the ankle.

Hawk put his lantern down and pushed cautiously at the
slabs, but they wouldn't budge. He took hold of the girl's
shoulders and pulled until his arms ached, but she didn't

budge either. The stones weren't going to give her up that easily. Hawk let go of her, and tried to think. The air was full of dust, and he coughed hard to try and clear it from his throat. The side of his face grew uncomfortably warm from having the lantern so close, and he moved it a bit further away. Shadows leapt alarmingly in the cramped tunnel and then were still again. He scowled, and worried his lower lip between his teeth. He had to get the child out of there. The tunnel could collapse at any time, bringing tons of stone and timber crashing down on her. And him too, for that matter. But there was no way he could persuade the stone slabs to give up their hold on her foot. He had no tools to work with, and even if he had, there wasn't enough room to apply any leverage. No, there was only one way to get the child out. Tears stung his eyes as the horror of it clenched at his gut, but he knew he had to do it. He didn't have any choice in the matter.

He squirmed and wriggled as best he could in the confined space, and finally managed to draw the knife from his boot and slide his leather belt out of his trousers. There was a good edge on the blade. It would do the job. He took a close look at the stone slabs where they held the child's foot, checking if there was room enough to work, but he already knew the answer. There was room. He was just putting it off. He looped his belt around the girl's leg, close up against the stone, and pulled it tight, until flesh bulged thickly up on either side of it. Hawk hefted the knife, and then brushed the little girl's hair gently with his free hand.

"Don't wake up, lass. I'll be as quick as I can."

He placed the edge of the knife against her leg, as close to the stones as he could get it, and began sawing.

There was a lot more blood than he'd expected, and he had to tighten the belt twice more before he could stem most of the flow. When he was finished, he tore off one of his sleeves and wrapped it tightly round the stump. His arms and face were splashed with blood, and he was breathing in great gulps, as though he'd just run a race. He turned over on his back again, grabbed his lantern, and began inching his way back down the tunnel, dragging the unconscious girl along behind him. He didn't know how long he'd spent in the narrow tunnel, but it felt like forever.

The tunnel roof soon rose enough to let him get to his hands and knees again, and he crawled along through the darkness, hugging the child to his chest. He suddenly found himself at the base of the main shaft, and stopped for a moment to get his breath. He ached in every muscle, and he'd torn his hands and knees to ribbons. But he couldn't let himself rest. The little girl needed expert medical help, and she was running out of time. He held the girl tightly to his chest with one arm and slowly began to climb back up the shaft, with only his legs and his back to support his weight and that of the child.

It didn't take long before the pain in his tired muscles became excruciating, but he wouldn't stop. The girl was depending on him. Foot by foot he fought his way up the shaft, grunting and snarling with the effort, his gaze fixed on the gradually widening circle of light above him. He finally drew near the surface, and eager hands reached down to take the child and help Hawk the rest of the way. He clambered laboriously out and lay stretched out on the rubble, squinting at the bright daylight and drawing in deep lungfuls of the comparatively clean air. Fisher swore softly at the state of his hands and knees, helped him sit up, and wrapped his cloak around him. Someone brought him a cup of lukewarm soup, and he sipped at it gratefully.

"The child," he said thickly. "What have they done with her?"

"A doctor's looking at her now," said Fisher. "And as soon as you've finished that soup we're going to get one to take a look at you, as well. God, you're a mess, Hawk. Was it bad down there?"

"Bad enough."

Eventually he got to his feet again, and Fisher found him a doctor who could work the right healing spells. The wounds closed up easily enough, but there was nothing the doctor could do for physical and emotional exhaustion. Hawk and Fisher looked around them. The dead and injured had been laid out in neat rows on the snow, the dying and the recovering lying side by side. A large pile of unidentified body parts had been tactfully hidden under a blood-spattered tarpaulin. Hawk shook his head numbly.

"All this, to catch one drug baron and his people. Tomorrow there'll be a dozen just like him fighting to take his place, and it will all have to be done again."

"Stop that," said Fisher sharply. "None of this is your fault. It's Morgan's fault, for having set up a pocket dimension here in the first place. And if we hadn't acted to stop the super-chacal being distributed, there's no telling how many thousands might have died across the city."

Hawk didn't answer. He looked slowly about him, taking in the situation. Engineers and sorcerers had got together to stabilize the surrounding buildings, and people were being allowed back into them again. That should please the slum landlords. Even they couldn't charge rent on a pile of rubble. Firemen were moving among the wreckage, shoring up the few broken walls and inner structures that hadn't collapsed completely. A few people were still sifting through the rubble, but the general air of urgency was gone. Much of the real work had been done now, and most people had accepted that there probably weren't going to be any more survivors. The volunteers had gone home, exhausted, and Hawk felt he might as well do the same. There was nothing left for him to do, he was out on his feet, and it had to be well past the end of his double shift. He was just turning to Fisher to tell her it was time to go, when there was the sound of gentle flute music, and the dry, acid voice of the communications sorcerer filled his head.

Captains Hawk and Fisher, return to Guard Headquarters immediately. This order supersedes all other directives.

Hawk looked at Fisher. "Typical. Bloody typical. What the hell do they want now?"

"Beats me," said Fisher. "Maybe they want to congratulate us for finally nabbing Morgan. There are a lot of people at Headquarters who'll fight for the chance to ask him some very pointed questions."

Hawk sniffed. "With our luck, they'll probably screw it up in the Courts, and he'll plea-bargain his way out with a fine and a suspended sentence."

"Relax," said Fisher. "We got him dead to rights this time. What can possibly go wrong?"

"What do you mean, you let him go?" screamed Hawk. He lunged across the desk at Commander Glen, and Fisher had to use all her strength to hold him back. The Commander pushed his chair back well out of reach, and glared at them both.

"Control yourself, Captain! That's an order!"

"Stuff your order! Do you know how many people died so we could get that bastard?"

He finally realised he couldn't break free from Fisher without hurting her, and stopped struggling. He took a deep breath and nodded curtly to Fisher. She let go of him and stepped back a pace, still watching him warily. Hawk fixed Commander Glen with a cold, implacable glare. "Talk to me, Glen. Convince me there's some reason behind this madness. Or I swear I'll do something one of us will regret."

Commander Glen sniffed, and met Hawk's gaze unflinchingly. Glen was a tallish, blocky man in his late forties, with a permanent scowl and a military-style haircut that looked as though it had been shaped with a pudding bowl. He had large, bony hands and a mouth like a knife-cut. He'd spent twenty years in the Guard, and amassed a reputation for thief-taking unequalled in the Guard. He'd been day Commander for seven years, and ran his people like his own private army, demanding and getting complete obedience. Ordinarily, he didn't have to deal much with Hawk and Fisher, which suited all of them.

Glen pushed his chair forward, and leaned his elbows on the desk. "You want me to explain myself, Captain Hawk? Very well. Thanks to your going after Morgan without waiting for orders or a backup, we now find ourselves faced with major loss of life and destruction of property within the Devil's Hook. We still don't know exactly how many died because of your actions, but the current total is four hundred and six. The Hook's still in shock at the moment, but when they finally realise what's happened, and that the Guard was responsible, we're going to be facing riots it'll take half the Guard to put down! On top of that, there's the cost of rebuilding and repairs, which is going to run into thousands of ducats. The landlord of the tenement is suing the Guard for that money, and he'll probably win. And finally, you assaulted a gang leader in front of his own people. Does the word *vendetta* mean anything to you, Captain Hawk?"

"I don't give a damn about any of that," said Hawk, his voice carefully controlled. "What I did was justified by the circumstances. Morgan was preparing to distribute a drug that would have killed thousands of people and torn Haven apart. Now, explain to me, please, why this man was allowed to go free."

"There was no evidence against him," said Glen flatly.

"No evidence? What about the super-chacal?" said Fisher. "There were crates of the damn stuff; I helped number and label them."

"I never saw any drugs," said Glen. "Neither has anyone else. And none of the prisoners had any drugs in their possession when they were searched here. None of them had even heard of this super-chacal you keep mentioning. And thanks to your efforts, we don't even have any proof the pocket dimension ever existed. That leaves only your word and that of your men. And that's not good enough, against someone like Morgan. He's a man of standing in the business community, and a pillar of society. He also has a great many friends in high places. People with influence. He hadn't been in Headquarters ten minutes before pressure began coming down from Above. Without real evidence, we didn't have a case. So I let him go, along with all of his people. I might add that Morgan is strongly considering suing us for false arrest, and you in particular for assault. I can't believe you were stupid enough to hit him in front of witnesses."

For a while, none of them said anything. It was very quiet in Glen's office, the only sound the murmur of people going back and forth about their business in the corridors outside.

"There were crates of the drug," said Hawk finally. "If they've disappeared, it can only mean they vanished on their way here, or they were removed by people working inside Headquarters. Either way, we're talking about corrupt Guards. I demand an official investigation."

"You can demand anything you want; you won't get it."

"I want to talk to my men, the Constables who were with me on the raid."

"I'm afraid that's not possible. They've already been detailed to other duties. Haven't you got the picture yet, Captain? As far as our superiors are concerned, this whole incident is a major embarrassment, and they want it forgotten as soon as possible. You've got some very important people mad at you. At both of you. They're looking for scapegoats, and you're tailor-made to fill the bill."

"Let me see if I've got this straight," said Hawk, his voice dangerously calm. "Morgan has walked. So have all his people. And several tons of the most dangerous drug Haven has ever seen have gone missing. Have I missed anything?"

"Yes," said Glen. "I've been instructed to suspend both of you, indefinitely, while a number of official charges against you are investigated. Charges such as reckless endangering of life and property, disobeying orders, assaulting citizens without provocation, brutality, and possible collusion in a vendetta against a faultless pillar of society. That last was Morgan, in case you were wondering."

Hawk grabbed Glen's desk with both hands and threw it to one side. Papers flew on the air like startled birds as he grabbed two handfuls of Glen's uniform, picked him up, and slammed him against the nearest wall. He thrust his face close to the Commander's, until they were staring into each other's eyes.

"No one's suspending me, you son of a bitch! Those drugs are still out there, waiting to be distributed! They have to be found and seized, and I can't do that with both hands tied behind my back! Do you understand me?"

Glen looked over Hawk's shoulder at Fisher, standing by the overturned desk. "Call your partner off, Fisher."

She shrugged, and folded her arms. "This time, I think I agree with him. If I were you, I'd agree with him too. Hawk can get very upset when he thinks people are conspiring against him."

The door burst open behind them and two Constables rushed in with drawn swords, alarmed at the sounds of violence from the Commander's office. Fisher drew her sword and quickly moved to stand between them and Hawk and Glen. Hawk slowly put Glen down, but kept a tight hold on him.

"Tell them to leave, Glen. This is private."

"Not anymore," said Glen. "Not after your foul-up this morning. You can't fight your way out of this one, Hawk. Not even you and Fisher can take on the entire Guard."

Hawk grinned suddenly. "Don't bet your life on it, Glen. We've faced worse odds in our time. Now, tell those overeager friends of yours to leave, and we'll ... discuss the situation."

He let go of Glen, and stepped back a pace, his right hand resting casually on the axe at his side. The Commander nodded, and gestured for the two Constables to leave. They looked at each other, shrugged, put away their swords and left, not quite slamming the door behind them. Glen looked at Hawk.

"You've upset them."

"Oh dear," said Hawk. "What a pity. I'm not going on suspension, Glen. I've got too much to do."

"Right," said Fisher.

"Help me pick up my desk," said Glen, "and we'll talk about it."

Hawk did so, while Fisher leaned against the wall, still holding her sword. Glen picked up his chair, and sat down behind his desk again. He glanced briefly at the papers scattered over the floor, then fixed his attention on Hawk and Fisher.

"All right, no suspension. But I'll have to find somewhere to put you so you're out of sight until things calm down again."

"Sounds sensible," said Fisher. "What did you have in mind?"

"I can't have you working together; word would be bound to get out. But as it happens, I've got two jobs to fill that should suit the pair of you nicely. As you know, even though officially you shouldn't, Peace Talks are taking place in Haven at the moment, to try and put an end to the border clashes between the Low Kingdoms and our traditional enemy Outremer, before they get out of hand. The Talks themselves seem to be going well enough, but there are a number of political and business interests on both sides who would like very much to see them fail. Captain David ap Owen is currently in charge of security, but he's been under a lot of pressure and could use some assistance. Think you could handle that, Captain Fisher?"

"Sounds fair enough to me," said Fisher, glancing at Hawk. "What level of security are we talking about?"

"Absolute minimum. Officially, the Talks aren't happening here at all. We can't use troops to guard the delegates; that would be too conspicuous, so there'll just be yourself, Captain ap Owen, and a dozen Constables in plainclothes. We can't use any magical protection, either. Same reason; it would just attract attention. So if anything happens, you're on your own. By the time you could get word to us it would all be over, one way or the other. You'll have to cope with what you've got."

"Do the delegates know that?" said Hawk.

"They suggested it. They're expendable, and they know it. Well, Captain Fisher, is the assignment to your liking?"

"Sounds like fun," said Fisher.

Glen looked at her for a moment, and then turned to Hawk. "I need someone to find the drugs that went missing. Surprisingly enough, I had worked out for myself

how dangerous this super-chacal could be. I want to know
how the stuff disappeared, and where it is now. And if you
should find a way to incriminate Morgan in the process, I
wouldn't be at all displeased. Find yourself another partner,
someone you can trust, but keep your head down, and stay
out of the public eye. If anything goes wrong, I'll swear
blind you were acting on your own, and it's all nothing
to do with me. I can't afford to have Morgan's friends as
enemies. You'll report directly to me, and no one else. Is
that acceptable, Captain Hawk?"

"Sounds good to me," said Hawk. "Why didn't you tell
us this earlier?"

"You didn't exactly give me a chance. You were more
interested in feeling aggrieved and wrecking my office."

Fisher smiled. "Next time, talk faster."

"Besides," said Hawk comfortingly, "it wasn't much of
an office anyway."

Glen looked at him.

Hawk was working on his second beer when Captain Burns
found him. The Cloudy Morning was a semiofficial off-duty
tavern for the Guard, a traditional place for winding down
at the end of a long shift. It was fairly basic as taverns go,
with no frills and few comforts, but the beer was good and
reasonably cheap, and the Guards needed a place where
they could talk freely without having to worry about who
might be listening. The place was run by an ex-Guard, and
the general public were politely encouraged to drink else-
where, unless they were Guard groupies. There were such,
though not many Guards encouraged them. They tended to
get obsessive.

The place was crowded, as usual at the end of a shift,
and Captain Burns had to squeeze his way through the
press of bodies to reach the bar. Several Guards called out
to him, and clapped him on the shoulder as he passed, but he
just smiled and kept going. Hawk's message had sounded
fairly urgent. He finally reached the bar, grabbed a seat as
it became vacant, and sat down beside Hawk. For a moment
Hawk didn't look up, staring into his beer. Then he took a

long swallow, and gestured for the bartender to bring Burns a beer.

"I'm surprised you're still on the loose," said Burns. "The smart money was betting you'd be arrested the moment you set foot in Headquarters. You've upset some really powerful people this time, Hawk."

"There was some talk of suspension," said Hawk. "But I talked the Commander out of it."

Burns smiled. "Yeah, I heard. Did you really bounce him off the walls of his own office?"

Hawk looked at him innocently. "Would I do such a thing to a superior officer?"

Burns nodded to the bartender as his drink arrived, and sipped it appreciatively. "So what's happening with you and Fisher? All forgiven?"

"Hardly. We've been split up, and told to keep our heads down. But I've got a case to work on, and I'm looking for a new partner."

For a moment, Burns didn't get it, and then he looked sharply at Hawk. "You mean me? We hardly know each other."

"I've seen you fight, and I thought you might like a chance to get back at the bastards who killed your partner. Besides, Morgan isn't going to stop with Fisher and me. Eventually, he's going to go after everyone who helped destroy his factory. He takes setbacks personally. If you don't go after him now, while he's vulnerable, you can bet that sooner or later he's going to be coming after you."

"You've got a point there," said Burns. "But you've got a real nerve, you know that? You got me into this mess, and now I'm supposed to help save your neck."

"Are you in or not?"

"Of course I'm in. I don't really have any choice, do I? And you're right about one thing, at least. I'd worked with Doughty on and off for nearly eight years. He was a good partner. Never had much to say for himself, but the best damned swordsman I ever saw. I always felt safer with him to guard my back. I didn't see who killed him at the factory. Everything was happening too fast. But even if I didn't see whose hand held the sword, I know who was responsible for his death."

"Morgan."

"Right. I'm with you, Hawk. But it's not going to be easy. Morgan has influential friends. The kind of people it's dangerous to cross."

"Everyone keeps telling me that," said Hawk calmly. "It's not going to stop me. I can be dangerous too, when I put my mind to it. But I shouldn't worry about his precious friends too much. If we bring Morgan down hard enough, his friends will desert him like rats leaving a sinking ship rather than risk being brought down with him."

Burns shook his head amusedly. "You almost make it sound easy. All right, what do we do first?"

"Well, to begin with we could do with another drink. We've got some hard thinking to do."

Burns chose his words carefully. "Not for me, thanks. I think better on a clear head."

"You're probably right," said Hawk. "But it has to be said, there's something about Haven that drives a man to drink." He looked at his empty glass, then pushed it regretfully away. "You know, when I first joined the Guard, I really thought I could make a difference. I was going to be a force for justice, and put all the bad guys behind bars, where they belonged. It didn't work out that way. Crime and corruption are a way of life for most people here. Some days I think the only way to clean up Haven would be to burn it down and start over again."

Burns shrugged. "I've lived here all my life, but from what I've heard, Haven isn't really that different from any other city. We're just more honest about it here. You mustn't let it get to you, Hawk. You can't expect to undo centuries of corruption overnight. Real change always takes time. In the meantime, we do our best to hold things together, and every now and again we get a chance to put away a piece of slime like Morgan. Settle for that."

They sat for a while in silence, each thinking his own thoughts.

"Where did you come from originally?" said Burns.

"Up North. There were family problems over my marriage to Isobel, so we struck out on our own. Travelled around a lot, and finally ended up here. It seemed a good idea at the time."

"There are worse places than Haven."

"Name two." Hawk looked thoughtfully into his empty glass. "It was my fault, you know. If I hadn't gone barging in, without checking the situation properly, I might have found a way to shut down Morgan's factory without destroying everything. And all those men and women and children would be alive now."

"Maybe," said Burns. "But I doubt it. Morgan was ready to ship those drugs out. If we'd burst in even an hour later, we'd probably have found nothing but an empty warehouse. But either way, it doesn't make any difference. You did what you thought was right at the time. That's all any of us can do. Beyond a certain point, worrying about past mistakes just becomes self-pity and self-indulgence."

Hawk looked at him, and smiled. "Maybe. Let's talk about Morgan, the bastard. The first thing we have to do is figure out where the super-chacal disappeared to, and then try and link it directly to Morgan in a way he can't shrug off. Which means asking pointed questions and making a nuisance of ourselves until people tell us what we want to know."

"Just once," said Burns, "wouldn't you like to try it the easy way? Morgan is going to have to shift the super-chacal in a hurry, so that he can't be caught with it in his possession. Which means using established channels of distribution. And there aren't that many people in Haven who can handle a deal that size. All we have to do is discover which distributor has suddenly become very busy, and we'll have our first lead."

"But that's only part of it," said Hawk. "We also need to know which Guards took money from Morgan to look the other way while the drugs went missing."

"If you say so," said Burns. "But Hawk, we're going to do this professionally, right? Getting personally involved in a case is always a bad idea. It stops you thinking clearly. In Haven, you win some and you lose some. That's just the way it is."

Hawk looked at him. "I don't believe in losing."

3

Talking Peace and War

Fisher strode scowling through the well-ordered streets of Low Tory, and wished Hawk was with her. She didn't like leaving him alone in his present mood. He'd taken the deaths in the Hook personally, and right now he was mad enough and depressed enough to do something stupid. Usually it was the other way round, with Hawk keeping her from doing something dumb, but there were times when he needed her to see the right path clearly. He needed her now, and she couldn't be with him. Commander Glen had made it very clear that their splitting up was a condition of their continuing to work. Still, they'd had time to discuss who Hawk should choose as his new partner, and Captain Burns seemed solid enough. She wondered what her own new partner would be like. Probably turn out to be some ex-mercenary with more muscle than brain, and even less ethics. There were a lot like that in the Guard.

She looked unobtrusively about her as she strode along, trying to get the feel of the new area. She hadn't worked Low Tory before, but by all accounts it was an upwardly mobile, middle-class area, full of merchant families so long established they were city aristocracy in all but blood and breeding. They were indecently rich, had a finger in every political pie, and, as a class, showed all the ethical restraint of a shark in a feeding frenzy. Having reached the pinnacle of their profession, their ambition turned in the only direction left to them, and they set their sights on the Quality. Even in Haven, the poorest aristocrat could still look down his nose at the richest trader. So, in recent times certain wealthy merchant families had been negotiating marriage contracts with the more impoverished Quality Families, quite openly offering to pay off a Family's debts in return for marriage into the Quality. The results were rarely happy, with the nouveau Quality snubbed and openly mocked by High Society, but the practice persisted.

As a result, Low Tory had flourished in the past few years, tearing down the faded and crumbling houses of the lesser Quality and replacing them with grand new mansions that rivalled and occasionally even surpassed the old Family Halls and Granges of High Tory. The streets were wide and open and bordered with neat, orderly rows of specially imported trees. New walls had been replaced with newer walls carefully constructed to appear old and weathered. Everything had to look right. Unlike most of Haven, the streets were calm and quiet and practically deserted. Regular patrols by private guards and men-at-arms saw to that. Only those with approved business in the area were allowed to tarry in Low Tory. To Fisher, more used to the bustling crowds of the Northside, the streets appeared almost eerily deserted.

The recent snow had been shovelled aside into tidy piles at the street kerbs, but here and there small bands of workmen still struggled with the more stubborn drifts. Servants attired in finery more costly than that worn by some lower-class merchants hurried along, looking neither left nor right, bearing messages and business documents and an almost palpable sense of their own self-importance. Private guards patrolled in pairs, looking faintly embarrassed by their overelaborate uniforms. None of them looked particularly pleased to see Fisher. She ignored them all, and concentrated on the directions she'd been given. They'd seemed simple enough back at Guard Headquarters, but Fisher had a positive genius for getting lost, and today seemed no different. Still, after a certain ammount of backtracking she'd finally found the right street, so all she had to do now was locate the right house.

It occurred to her that this street was actually surprisingly busy, by Low Tory standards. There were half a dozen workmen lackadaisically shovelling snow, and as many servants strolling unhurriedly up and down the street. A hot-chestnut seller was tending his brazier, but showed remarkably little interest in drumming up trade. Two men were bent over an open sewer grating, but seemed to be spending as much time watching the street as anything else. Fisher had to smile. Try as they might, some Guards just couldn't get the hang of plainclothes work. It wasn't enough to look the part; you had to act it as well. Still, it showed she was in the right place.

None of the plainclothes people made any move to approach her, for which Fisher was grateful. She wasn't in the mood to explain what she was doing there without Hawk. She finally reached her destination, and stopped at the main gate to study the surroundings with an experienced eye. It was a plain, pleasantly unornamented house, standing a way back from the street in its own grounds. The high stone wall surrounding the snow-covered lawns was topped with iron spikes and broken glass. Fairly impressive, but the tall iron gates were unlocked and unguarded. She'd have to speak to someone about that.

She pushed the gates open and walked into the grounds. A few yards away stood a life-sized figure of a warrior, carved from pale marble in the classically idealized style popular in the last century. It carried a sword and shield, and was minutely detailed, even down to bulging veins on the muscular arms. Fisher looked away. She didn't care for such statues. They'd always given her the creeps as a child.

As she passed the marble warrior, there was a low, grating sound as the statue slowly turned its head and looked at her. Fisher jumped back, her hand dropping to her sword. She stayed where she was, her heart beating painfully fast, but the statue made no further move. Fisher edged closer, a foot at a time, and reached out to poke it with a hesitant fingertip. It felt hard and unyielding, the way marble should. Fisher took a deep breath and backed away, still keeping a careful eye on the statue. The thing must be part of the house's security system. They might have warned her. . . . She turned her back on the marble figure and continued on her way. Behind her she again heard a low grating sound as the statue turned its head to follow her progress. Fisher wouldn't let herself look back, but walked a little faster, despite herself. Up ahead, scattered across the grounds, were three more statues, staring off in different directions.

Snow crunched loudly under Fisher's boots as she approached the house. Now that she'd had a chance to get used to the idea, she approved of the statues. Simple but effective security, and completely unobtrusive until activated by an intruder. She couldn't help wondering what other surprises Captain ap Owen might have set up in the grounds. The thought had only just crossed her mind when a huge dog suddenly appeared out of nowhere right in front of her. She stumbled to a halt, and the great hound thrust its head forward, sniffed at her suspiciously, and then vanished into thin air. Fisher opened her mouth to say something, and a second, different dog appeared out of nowhere just to her left. It was even bigger than the first, its head on a level with her belt. It sniffed at her, wagged its tail, then snapped out of existence. Fisher realised her mouth was still hanging open, and shut it. Guard dogs. Of course. Entirely logical. She walked on, and tried to get her breathing to go back to normal.

She finally came to a halt before the massive front door, beat on it smartly with her fist, and made a quick use of the iron boot-scraper. *And if anything else appears, I'm going to hit it first, and ask questions afterwards.* The door opened almost immediately, confirming that they'd been watching her.

The man in footman's uniform looked convincing enough, and even had the barely civil bow and haughty expression down right, but there was no getting away from the fact that he was simply far too muscular for a gentleman's servant.

He stood back politely as she entered the brightly lit hall, then shut the door firmly behind her. The sound of a key turning in the lock was quickly followed by the sound of four separate bolts sliding home. Fisher smiled, and relaxed a little. Maybe they did know what they were doing here, after all. She handed the footman her cloak, waited patiently while he figured out where to hang it up, and then allowed him to lead her down the hall and into the study, where Captain David ap Owen was waiting for her.

The study was too large to be really cosy, but had all the comforts money could buy. Captain ap Owen sat behind a large, ornate desk, talking quietly to someone who looked as though he might be a real footman. Ap Owen glanced at Fisher as she came in, but finished giving his instructions before waving both footmen away. He got up from behind the desk and came forward to greet Fisher with an outstretched hand. His handshake was firm, but hurried, and he sat down on the edge of the desk to take a good look at her. Fisher stared back just as openly.

Captain ap Owen was in his mid-thirties, and a little less than average height, which meant he had to tilt his head back to meet her gaze. It didn't seem to bother him as much as it did some people. His build was stocky rather than muscular, and his uniform had a sloppy, lived-in look. Fisher approved of that. In her experience, Guards who worried too much about their appearence tended not to worry enough about getting the job done right. Ap Owen had flaming red hair and bright green eyes, along with a broad rash of freckles across his nose and cheekbones which made him look deceptively youthful and open. His apparently relaxed stance was undermined by an unwavering slight frown and occasional sudden, jerky movements. Even sitting still, he gave the impression of a man constantly on edge, just waiting for an attack so he could leap into action.

"Take a seat, Captain Fisher," he said finally. "Glad to have you with us. I've heard a lot about you."

"It's all true," said Fisher easily. She dragged a chair over to the desk, ignoring what that did to the carpet, and slumped gracelessly into it. The chair was a rickety antique, but more comfortable than it appeared. She looked sharply at ap Owen. "I take it you've heard the latest news about me?"

"Of course," said ap Owen. "If it hadn't been for your recent . . . troubles, I'd never have got you on my team. Make no mistake, Captain, everyone here, including you and me and the six delegates, are all considered expendable. If these Talks work out successfully, fine; if not, no one's going to miss us. They'll just start over, with new delegates and new Talks. The odds are we're all going to be killed before the Talks are over. There are a lot of people out there who want us dead, for various political and business reasons, and I haven't been allowed enough men to ward off a determined attack by a group of lightly armed nuns. Had to be that way. The whole idea of this operation is to be unobtrusive and hopefully overlooked. Personally, I think it's a dumb idea, given the number of spies and loose mouths in this city, but no one asked my opinion. The point is that if things go wrong and our cover is blown, we are supposed to defend these Talks with our lives, and we probably will. Even though they and we are completely replaceable."

"I see you're the kind of leader who believes in a good pep talk," said Fisher. "Are you normally this optimistic?"

Captain ap Owen grinned briefly. "I like my people to know what they're getting into. Ideally, this should have been a volunteers-only operation, but since we couldn't tell them what they'd be volunteering for, there didn't seem much point. How much did they tell you about our situation here?"

"Not much. Just that it was minimum security, with essentially no backup."

"You got that right, but it's not quite as bad as it sounds. The Talks aren't actually taking place in the house itself, the building's far too vulnerable. Instead, a Guard sorcerer has set up a pocket dimension, linked to the house. It's been so thoroughly warded, a sorcerer could walk through this place from top to bottom and never know the dimensional gateway was here. Clever, eh?"

"Very," said Fisher carefully. "But pocket dimensions aren't exactly stable, are they? If you know about my current problems, then you can understand that I'm a bit bloody wary about going into another pocket dimension."

"Don't worry about it; once the dimension's been established, it's perfectly secure. The only reason Morgan's fell apart is because he designed it that way, with booby traps in case he was discovered. He didn't want any evidence surviving to incriminate him."

Fisher looked at him blankly. "You mean it wasn't Hawk's fault after all? Then why didn't Commander Glen tell us that? He must have known . . . Damn, I've got to talk to Hawk!"

She jumped to her feet, but ap Owen didn't budge. "Sit down, Captain Fisher. You're not going anywhere. No one here is allowed to leave these premises until the Talks are over. It's a matter of security. You must see that."

"You can't stop me leaving."

"No, I probably couldn't. But if you did leave, Glen would undoubtedly have you declared a rogue, and put out an order for your arrest. And how is that going to help Hawk?"

Fisher glared at ap Owen, then nodded reluctantly and sank back into her chair. "That's why Glen sent me here, so Hawk would be left alone with his guilt. He's always easiest to manipulate when he's feeling guilty. Glen wants Hawk to go on believing it was his fault, so he'll be properly motivated to go after Morgan. Damn him!"

There was an uncomfortable silence. When Fisher finally spoke again, her voice was calm and cold and very deadly. "When this is all over, there's going to be an accounting between me and Commander bloody Glen."

"Assuming we get out of this alive," said ap Owen.

Fisher glanced at him sharply. "You're a real cheerful sort, you know that?"

"Just being realistic. Let me fill you in on the six delegates taking part in the Talks. They're a pretty rum bunch themselves, particularly the Outremer delegates. They were mad as hell when they arrived. Apparently it took them the best part of five weeks to get here through the winter weather, and that was before the worst of the storms hit. I don't see why they couldn't have just teleported in."

"Teleports don't work that way," said Fisher. "It's hard enough to shift one person over a short distance. There isn't a sorcerer alive with the kind of magic it would take to teleport three people from one country to another. There are lots of nasty ways for a teleport to go wrong. Get the decimal point in the wrong place and you could end up appearing a hundred feet above your destination. Or under it."

"I didn't realise you were such an expert," said ap Owen dryly.

Fisher shrugged. "I've had some experience with travelling that way."

"Actually, the weather is something of a blessing. The storms are keeping Outremer's more disruptive elements from getting here. Let's just hope the storms continue till the Talks are over."

"Maybe someone should have a word with the city weather wizards."

"No, low profile, remember? Nothing that would attract attention."

"True. All right, tell me about the delegates. Who's representing the Low Kingdoms? Anyone I might have heard of?"

"Maybe. Lord Regis is heading the home team. This is his house we're in. Mid-forties, old Haven Family, good reputation, with an impressive background in the army and the diplomatic corps. Can't say I warm to him myself. Smiles too much, and takes too long to shake your hand. Likes to clap you on the shoulder while looking you right in the eye. Hail-fellow-well-met type. He gets on my nerves something fierce, but he goes down well enough with the other delegates.

"Then there's Jonathon Rook, representing the Merchants Association. Early forties, and better padded than the average sofa. He likes his food, does Jonathon. Sharp as a tack when it comes to business, but he does love a title. Practically milorded Regis to death this morning, while we were waiting for the Outremer delegates to show up. Word is he's angling for a Family marriage for his eldest, more fool he.

"And finally, there's Major Patrik Comber. You've probably heard of him. Led his battalion into Death's Hollow to rescue a company of his men who'd been cut off by Outremer troops. Took on better than five-to-one odds, and kicked their arses something cruel. Won all sorts of medals, and a swift promotion. He also sacrificed a lot of good men in the process, but the minstrels don't usually mention that."

Fisher grinned. "I can see you're going to be a real barrel of laughs on this job. How about the Outremer delegates? Do you like them any better?"

"Not much. The leader is Lord Nightingale. Pleasant enough sort, but I don't think I'll turn my back on him. He's got cold eyes. Then there's William Gardener for the merchants, and Major Guy de Tournay. Can't tell you much about them. Gardener likes his drink and talks too loudly, while de Tournay's hardly opened his mouth to me since he got here."

Fisher frowned thoughtfully. "Interesting that both sides have put forward a lord. The Quality aren't normally considered expendable. Particularly not someone as noticeable as Lord Regis. And from what I've heard, Major Comber's something of a popular hero at the moment. The Powers That Be Must be taking these Talks pretty seriously."

"Seems likely. Both sides have been losing a lot of men and equipment in the border skirmishes, and it's getting expensive. You know how the Powers That Be hate to lose money. Of course, they hate to lose face even more, which is why it's taken till now to set the Talks up."

"All right. Fill me in on what security measures you've set up here. If we're not allowed to call attention to ourselves, it cuts our options down to practically nothing, doesn't it?"

"You've got that right," said ap Owen grimly. "For all the good we'd be in a real crisis, we might as well not be here. I take it you spotted the plainclothes people outside? I'd be surprised if you hadn't; everyone else knows who and what they are. Luckily, they're just out there for show. My real undercover operatives have been here for days, establishing their characters and getting to know the area. We didn't just choose this place on a whim, you know. Both the grounds and the surrounding streets are wide open, with nowhere to hide. The way we've got things set up, no one can get within a hundred yards of this house without being spotted a dozen times. And since we haven't a hope in hell of beating off an armed assault, at the first whisper of an attack, or even an intended attack, the plan is for all of us to retreat into the pocket dimension and seal it off.

"In theory, we should then be perfectly safe. No one can get at us without the proper co-ordinates, known only to a top few people, so all we have to do is sit tight and wait until reinforcements arrive, and the emergency is over. Of course, there's always the very real possibility that the delegates themselves will seal off the dimension at the first whiff of trouble, leaving us out here to fight off the attackers. In which case, we get to earn our money the hard way. Got it?"

Fisher nodded glumly. In other words, it was another damned watching brief. Lots of sitting around doing nothing, waiting for something to happen and hoping it wouldn't. It was at times like these that Fisher seriously considered the simple pleasures of a desk job, and the security to be found in lots of nice safe paperwork. Of course, she'd be bored out of her mind in a week . . . Ah well, if nothing else, she should be able to catch up on her sleep here. Working two shifts in a row had drained most of her strength, and helping Hawk drag survivors out of the tenement rubble had all but finished her off. She felt as if she could go to sleep right there in her chair. She caught herself slumping forward, and quickly sat up straight. Almost without realising it, her eyes had been closing, and she'd actually come close to nodding off. That would have made a great first impression on Captain ap Owen. She glanced quickly at him to see if he'd noticed anything, but he was apparently absorbed in leafing through the papers on his desk.

"Tell me about the Talks themselves," she said, to show she was still with it. "Are they making any progress?"

"Beats me. I'm just the hired help round here; no one tells me anything. I'm not even allowed into the pocket dimension unless one of them calls for me, and though the delegates take an occasional break out here, none of them are much for small talk. As far as I can discover, their brief is to agree on a border frontier both sides can live with, and put an end to all those squabbles over which ragged old piece of map takes precedence. Both the Low Kingdoms and Outremer are going to end up losing some territory, so both sides are throwing in lucrative trade deals as sweeteners to help the medicine go down. Whatever happens, you can bet a lot of people living near the border will wake up one morning to find that overnight they've become citizens of a different country. Poor bastards. Probably end up paying two sets of taxes."

Fisher frowned. "Those special trade deals are going to put a lot of noses out of joint in the business community. Nothing like a little preferential treatment to stir up bad feelings."

"Right," said ap Owen. "And let's not forget, there's a hell of a lot of money to be made out of a war, if you've got the right kind of contacts with the military."

"Any more bad news you'd like to share with me?"

"You mean apart from political extremists, religious fanatics, and terrorists-for-hire?"

"Forget I asked. Do you think it'll come to a war, if the Talks fail?"

"I don't know . . . Countries have gone to war over a lot less in the past. The Low Kingdoms have traditionally preferred action to talk, and Outremer can be touchy as hell where its honour is concerned. I wouldn't be surprised if a war did break out, but then it must be said I have something of a vested interest in war. I've always made most of my living as a mercenary. I only ended up as a Guard because

I'd spent too long between jobs and the money had run out. Ironic, really, that I should end up protecting Talks whose purpose is to keep me and my kind out of work. You ever been caught up in a war, Captain Fisher?"

"Just once," said Fisher. "Several years back. It's funny, you know; at the time I would have given everything I owned to be somewhere else, somewhere safe. But now, looking back, it seems to me I've never felt so alive as I did then. We were fighting for great stakes, and everything I did mattered; everything I did was important. But I wouldn't go through it again for all the money in the Low Kingdoms' Treasury. I saw too many good people die, saw too many people I cared for hurt and maimed."

"Did you win?"

"Yes and no." Fisher smiled tiredly. "I suppose that's true of any war. Our side won in the end, but the Land was devastated by the fighting. It'll take generations to recover. I suppose you've seen a lot of war, as a mercenary?"

Ap Owen shrugged. "More than I care to remember. One war is much like another, and the campaigns all tend to blur into each other after a while. Endless marching, rotten food, and lousy weather. Waiting for orders that never come, in some godforsaken spot in the middle of nowhere. And every now and again, just often enough to keep your nerves ragged, there'll be a sudden burst of action. You get used to the blood and the flies and seeing your comrades die, and there's always the looting to look forward to afterwards. I could have been a rich man a dozen times over, if I could have kept away from the cards and the dice and the tavern whores. I started out fighting for a cause, but that didn't last long. First thing you learn as a mercenary is that both sides believe they're right.

"So why have I spent most of my adult life fighting for strangers? Because I'm good at it. And because, just as you said, you never feel more alive than when you've just cheated death. In its way, that feeling's more addictive than any drug you'll find on the streets." He broke off, and smiled at Fisher. "You're a good listener, Fisher, you know that?"

Before she could say anything, a ring on ap Owen's finger pulsed with a sudden silver light, and he rose quickly to his feet. "That's the delegates' signal; they're going to take another break. Just stay back out of the way, for the time being. I'll introduce you if I get a chance, but don't expect any great show of interest. We're just hired help as far as they're concerned."

Two footmen entered the study in response to some unheard summons, carrying silver trays laden with assorted delicacies of the kind Fisher hadn't seen in the markets for weeks. Whoever was funding these Talks obviously didn't believe in doing things by halves. The footmen put down their trays on the main table, by the cut-glass wine decanters, then withdrew without saying a word. Fisher decided they were probably real footmen, if only because of their supercilious expressions.

Ap Owen stood before his desk, staring at the far wall. Fisher followed his gaze, but couldn't see anything of interest. She started to ask something, and then shut up as a door appeared out of nowhere, hanging unsupported on the air a few inches above the floor. It was plain, unvarnished wood, without pattern or trimmings, but its very presence was subtly disturbing. A mounting chill emanated from it, like a cold wind blowing into the room. Fisher's hand dropped to her sword, and she had to fight to keep from drawing it as the door swung slowly open.

The delegates appeared through the doorway, chatting quietly together, and headed for the food and wine without so much as a glance at ap Owen and Fisher. The door shut silently, and disappeared. Fisher took her hand away from her sword. Ap Owen moved in beside her and quietly identified each delegate by name. Fisher looked them over carefully without being too obvious about it.

Lord Regis of Haven was of average height and weight, and in pretty good shape for a man in his early fifties. He had dark, flashing eyes and a quick smile buried in a neatly trimmed beard. He used his hands a lot as he talked, and nodded frequently while he listened. Lord Nightingale of Outremer was twenty years younger, six inches taller, and muscular in a broad, solid way that suggested he lifted weights on a regular basis. Which was a little unusual. As far as most of the Quality were concerned, strenuous exercise was something best left to the lower classes. The Quality only exerted themselves in duelling or seducing. Usually both, as one often led to the other. Nightingale, on the other hand, looked as though he could have picked up Regis with one hand, and torn him apart with the other. If Regis was aware of this, it didn't seem to bother him.

The two traders, Rook and Gardener, were talking together quite amicably, smiling and laughing as they rummaged through the out-of-season delicacies on the trays. Fisher's stomach rumbled, but she made herself pay attention to the two merchants. William Gardener of Outremer was in his early forties, with thinning hair and a droopy moustache. He was skinny as a rake, but wore clothes of the very latest cut with casual elegance. Jonathon Rook was the same age, and dressed just as well, but had the kind of figure politely referred to as stout. His hands were weighed down with jewelled rings, and he paid little or no attention to the expensive food with which he was stuffing his face. Fisher moved in a little closer to listen in on their conversation. They both studiously ignored her, which suited her fine. It soon became clear that both merchants thought they had a lot to lose in the event of a war, and were pressing for peace at practically any cost. It was also clear they were finding it an uphill struggle.

Major Comber and Major de Tournay stood a little way off from the others, talking quietly and only picking at their food. They were both in their late thirties, with short-cropped hair and grim faces. They'd swapped their uniforms for civilian clothes, and Fisher was hard put to tell which of them looked the most uncomfortable. They both glared at her when she got too close, so she didn't get to overhear what they were saying. She sensed, however, that neither one was too pleased with the way the Talks were going, from which she deduced that neither side had gained the upper hand yet.

They all finally put down their plates and turned away

from the table. Captain ap Owen coughed loudly, and then again, louder still, and having got their attention, introduced Fisher to each of them. Fisher bowed formally, and got a series of perfunctory nods in reply. Lord Regis smiled at her coldly.

"Good to have you with us, Captain. Your reputation precedes you."

"You don't want to believe everything you hear," said Fisher easily. "Only the bad bits."

Regis smiled politely. "Is your partner, Captain Hawk, not here with you?"

"He's working on a case of his own at the moment, and can't leave it, I'm afraid. But not to worry, my lord. You're safe in our hands."

"I'm sure we shall be."

"I trust you'll pardon my interruption," said Lord Nightingale, looking only at Lord Regis, "but we are rather short of time. Perhaps you could continue this conversation later . . ."

"Of course," said Regis.

He nodded politely to Fisher and ap Owen, and turned to face the far wall. The door reappeared, and swung silently open. Fisher shivered suddenly. She tried to see what lay beyond the door, but there was only an impenetrable darkness. The delegates filed through, and the door swung shut behind them and vanished. Fisher sank back into her chair and stretched out her legs. This was going to be a long, hard job, she could tell. She looked thoughtfully at the food left on the table, but didn't have the energy to get up and go after it. She hoped Hawk was taking it easy, wherever he was, but doubted it. Without her to keep an eye on him, there was no telling what he'd get up to.

4

A Matter of Trust

Hawk led Captain Burns into the rotten heart of the Northside. The streets grew steadily narrower, choked with filthy snow and slush, and bustling crowds that made way for the two Guards without ever looking at them directly. Even so, they made slow progress, and Hawk had to fight to control his impatience. The pressure seemed to be bearing down on him from every side now, but he knew his only hope of dealing with it was to stay clam and controlled. His enemies would be delighted to see him striking out blindly in all directions and missing the real targets. Besides, he didn't want to spook Burns. And yet behind his grim, impassive face, Hawk's thoughts danced restlessly from one problem to another, searching for answers that eluded him. The super-chacal was out there somewhere, poised to sweep across the city in a tidal wave of blood and death. Morgan was out there too, hidden somewhere safe and plotting the deaths of everyone who knew the truth about his new drug. Not to mention Hammer, the gang leader from the Devil's Hook, and his threatened vendetta.

And also back at the Hook, the little girl Hawk had rescued from underneath the wreckage was lying in a hospital bed, still in a coma. The doctors didn't know whether she'd ever regain consciousness.

On top of all that, the Guard wanted his scalp for screwing up, and they'd taken Isobel away from him. Some days you just couldn't get a break. Hawk realised Burns was speaking to him, and looked round sharply.

"I'm sorry. What?"

"I said," Burns repeated patiently, "is it always this bad here? I'd heard stories, of course, but this place is disgusting."

Hawk looked around at the squalid buildings and the ragged people, and the overriding sense of violence and despair that rose from them like an almost palpable mist. After five years working the Northside he'd grown inured to most of the misery and suffering, for the sake of his sanity, but it still disturbed him enough to appreciate how bad it must seem to an outsider. Haven was a dark city wherever you looked, but the Northside was dark enough to stamp out the light in anyone's soul eventually. Hawk realised Burns was still looking at him for an answer, and he shrugged harshly.

"It's quiet today, if anything. The snow and the cold are keeping most people off the streets, even the beggars, and those who are out and about aren't hanging around long enough to start any trouble. But you can bet that somewhere, someone is starting a fight, or stabbing someone in the back for no good reason. There's all sorts of crime here, everything you'd expect in an area as poor as this, but the violence never ends. To a Northsider, everyone is an enemy, out to steal what little he has, and most of the time he's right. There's little love or comfort here, Burns, and even less hope. And the only thing the Northsiders hate more than each other is an outsider. Like us."

"How do you cope with working here?" said Burns. "I'd go crazy in a week."

Hawk shrugged. "I've seen worse. All you can do is try and make a difference for the best, where you can. What brought you here from the Westside?"

"Doughty and I were filling in for some Guards who were down with the flu. When I heard they were sending us here, I seriously thought about calling in sick myself, but of course it was too late by then. Doughty didn't mind. There wasn't much that bothered him."

"I'm sorry about your partner," said Hawk.

"Yeah. He had a wife, you know. Separated three years back, but . . . Someone will have told her by now. I should have done it myself, but she never liked me anyway."

They walked in silence for a while, not looking at each other.

"So, what's the plan?" said Burns finally. "Are we headed anywhere in particular?"

"I thought we'd start off with Short Tom," said Hawk. "Has a nice little distribution setup, down on Carlisle Street. He'll move anything for anyone, as long as the money's right. Not one of the biggest, but certainly one of the longest established. I doubt he's handling the super-chacal himself, but he'll probably have a damned good idea who might be."

"Will he talk to us? Do you have a good relationship with him?"

Hawk looked at Burns. "This is the Northside, no one here talks to the Guard willingly. We're the enemy, the ones who enforce the laws that keep them in their place. The poverty here's so bad, most people will do anything to escape it. They don't care who they rob or who they hurt. All they care about is making that one big score that will finally get them out of the Northside. You can't reason with people like that. Short Tom will talk to me because he knows what will happen to him if he doesn't."

Burns stared straight ahead of him, his face expressionless. "I don't approve of strong-arm tactics. I put on this uniform to help people, not oppress them."

"You've spent too long in the Westside, Burns. They still like to pretend they're living in a civilised city over there. Here in the Northside, they'd quite happily cut you down for the loose change in your pockets, or a chance at your boots. The only thing that keeps them off my back is the certain knowledge that I'll kill them if they even think of raising a hand against me. I have to be obviously more dangerous than they are at all times, or I'd be a dead man. Look . . . I used to think the same as you, once.

There are good people here, same as there are good people everywhere, and I do my best to help and protect them. Even if it means bending or ignoring the rules to do so. But when you get right down to it, my job is to enforce the law. Whatever it takes."

"Being the Guard doesn't give us the right to beat up someone just because we think they might have information that might help us. There are procedures, proper ways of doing things."

Hawk sighed. "I know. I've read the Manual too. But the procedures take time, and for all I know, the super-chacal's already seeping out onto the streets. I could threaten to arrest Short Tom, maybe even drag him down to Headquarters and throw him in a cell to think things over. But I couldn't hold him for long, and he knows it. I don't have the time to be a nice guy about this, and to be blunt, I don't have the inclination. My way works, and I'll settle for that. I've never laid a finger on an innocent man, or killed a man who didn't deserve it."

"How can you be sure? How can you be sure you haven't killed an innocent man by accident? The dead can't defend themselves from other people's accusations. We're Captains in the Guard, Hawk—not judge, jury, and executioner."

"I go by what works," said Hawk flatly. "When the people in the Northside start playing by the rules, so will I. Look, there are just four Captains and a dozen Constables to cover the whole Northside. We can't be everywhere at once, so we have to let our reputations go ahead of us. It's a big area, Burns, and rotten to the core. All we can ever hope to do is keep the lid on. Now, I don't care if you approve of how I do my job or not; just watch my back and don't interfere. The only thing that matters now is stopping Morgan and his stinking drug."

Burns nodded slowly. "Of course, finding the super-chacal would go a long way towards reinstating you in the Guard, wouldn't it?"

Hawk looked at him coldly. "If you think that's the only reason I'm doing this, then you don't know me at all."

"Sorry. You're right, of course. Hawk, can I ask you something . . . personal?"

"I don't know. Maybe. What?"

"What happened to your eye?"

"Oh, that. I pawned it."

Short Tom's place was a two-storey glorified lean-to, adjoining a battered old warehouse on Carlisle Street. The street itself was blocked from one end to the other by an open-air market and the tightly packed crowd it had drawn. The tattered, gaudy stalls crowded up against each other, and the vendors behind them filled the air with their aggressive patter. Most of them were bundled up to their ears in thick winter furs, but it didn't seem to be slowing them down any. Some of them were all but jumping up and down on the spot in their attempt to explain just how magnificent and amazingly affordable their goods were. Hawk glanced at a few stalls, but wasn't impressed. Still, with Haven's Docks closed by the winter storms, goods of all kinds were getting scarce, and even rubbish like this was starting to look good. The smell was pretty bad, particularly around the food stalls, and Burns pulled one face after another as he and Hawk made their way slowly through the crowd. Even their Guards' uniforms couldn't make them any room in such a crush.

Short Tom's lean-to loomed up before them, looking more and more unsafe the closer they got. It looked like it had been thrown together on the cheap by a builder in a hurry, trying to stay one step ahead of his reputation. The walls weren't straight, the wood was stained and warped, and the door and window frames were lopsided. It was a mess, even by Northside standards. Still, it was no doubt cheap to rent, and for a man in Short Tom's line of business, that was all that really mattered.

Two large bravos in heavy sheepskin coats stood before the main door, arms folded, glaring impartially about them. Hawk walked up to the one on the left, and punched him out. The second bravo yelped in disbelief and started to unfold his arms. Hawk kicked him in the knee, waited for him to bend forward, and then knocked him out with the butt of his axe. No one in the milling crowd paid any attention. It was none of their business. Burns looked at Hawk.

"Was that really necessary?"

"Yes," said Hawk. "They wouldn't have let us in without a fight, and if I'd given them a chance to draw their swords, someone would have got seriously hurt. Most probably them, but you never know. Now follow me, watch my back, and let me do all the talking. And try to at least look mean."

He stepped over the unconscious bravos, pushed open the door and stepped through, followed closely by Burns. Inside, all was surprisingly neat and tidy, with clerks sitting behind two rows of desks, shuffling pieces of paper and making careful entries in two sets of ledgers. One of the clerks shouted for them to shut the bloody door and keep the bloody cold out, and Burns quickly did so. Hawk glanced at him, and shook his head. Far too long in the Westside. He looked back at the clerks, who had finally realised who the newcomers were. One clerk opened his mouth to shout a warning.

"Don't," said Hawk.

The clerk looked at the axe in Hawk's hand, thought about it, and shut his mouth.

"Good boy," said Hawk. He looked about him, and the clerks shrank down behind their desks. Hawk smiled coldly. "My partner and I are going upstairs to have a nice little chat with Short Tom. Just carry on as normal. And by the way, if anyone was to come up after us and interrupt our little chat, I will be most upset. Is that clear?"

The clerks nodded quickly, and did their best to look as though the idea had never entered their heads. Hawk and Burns strolled casually between the desks and up the stairway at the back of the room. Burns watched the clerks' faces out of the corner of his eye. They'd all recognised Hawk by now, and there was real terror in their faces, and not a little awe. Burns frowned thoughtfully. He'd heard stories about Hawk—everyone had—but he'd never really believed them. Until now.

They found Short Tom in his office, right at the top of the stairs. It was a nice little place, neat and tidy and almost cosy, with thick rugs on the floor, comfortable furniture, and attractive watercolor landscapes on the walls. Short Tom looked up as they entered, and his face fell. Not surprisingly, given his name, he was a dwarf, with stubby arms and legs and a large head. He wore the very latest fashion, and it was a credit to his tailor that he didn't look any more ridiculous than anybody else. He was sitting at a normal-sized desk, on a custom-made chair, and he pushed it back slightly as he reached for a desk drawer.

"I wouldn't," said Hawk. "I really wouldn't."

Short Tom nodded glumly, and took his hand away from the drawer. "Captain Hawk. How nice to see you again. Absolutely marvelous. What do you want?"

"Just a little chat," said Hawk. "I've got a problem I thought you might be able to help me with."

"I'm clean," said Short Tom immediately. "One hundred per cent. I'm entirely legitimate these days."

"Of course you are," said Hawk. "In which case, you won't mind my bringing in the tax inspectors to go through all your invoices, will you?"

Short Tom sighed heavily. "What can I do for you, Captain?"

"Morgan's got a small mountain of drugs on his hands that he has to move in a hurry."

"He hasn't contacted me. I swear he hasn't."

"I know he hasn't. You're not big enough for this. But you can give me some names. With a deal this urgent, there's bound to have been talk already."

"I've heard about your run-in with Morgan," said Short Tom carefully, "and I can't afford to get involved. I'm just a small-time operator, dealing in whatever odds and ends the big boys can't be bothered with. As long as I know my place, no one bothers me. If I start talking out of turn, Morgan will send some of his heavies round to shut me up permanently. You'll have to find your help somewhere else."

"Thousands of people could die if we don't stop this drug hitting the street."

"That's not my problem."

Hawk raised his axe above his head and brought it sweeping down in one swift, savage movement. The axehead buried itself in Short Tom's desk, splitting the polished desktop apart. Hawk yanked the axe free and struck the desk again, putting all his strength into it. The desk caved in, sheared almost in two. Splinters flew on the air, and papers fluttered to the floor like wounded birds. Short Tom sat very still, looking down at the wreckage of his desk. He raised his eyes and looked at Hawk, standing before him with his axe at the ready.

"On the other hand," said Short Tom very politely, "I've always believed in co-operating with the forces of law and order whenever possible."

He came up with four names and addresses, all of which Hawk recognised. He nodded his thanks, and left. Burns hurried after him, having almost missed his cue. His last glimpse was of Short Tom staring glumly at what was left of his desk. Burns followed Hawk down the stairs and back through the rows of clerks, all of whom were careful to keep their eyes glued to their work as the Guards passed. Hawk and Burns stepped out into the street again, and Burns winced as the bitter cold hit him hard after the comfortable warmth of the offices. He stubbed his toe on something, and looked down to find the two bravos who'd guarded the front door still lying where they'd fallen. Only now they were stark-naked, having been stripped of everything they owned. Their flesh was a rather pleasant pale blue, set against the dirty grey of the snow. Hawk chuckled.

"That's the Northside for you."

"We can't just leave them like this," protested Burns. "They'll freeze to death."

"Yeah, I know. Give me a hand and we'll dump them back in the offices. Short Tom will take care of them. But let this be a lesson to you, Burns. Never give a Northsider an opening, or he'll steal you blind. And the odds are there's not one person in this crowd who would have lifted a finger to help these two bravos. They'd have just left them there to freeze. In the Northside, people learn from an early age not to care for anyone but themselves."

"Is that where you learned it?" said Burns.

Hawk looked at him, and Burns had to fight down an urge to look away from the glare of the single cold eye. When Hawk finally spoke, his voice was calm and unhurried.

"I think we're going to get on a lot better if you stop acting like a character from a religious pamphlet. I don't know how you've managed to survive this long in Haven; I can only assume they've had a hot flush of civilisation in the Westside since I was last there.

"Look, Burns, let's get this clear once and for all. I'm only as hard as I need to be to get the job done. I take no pleasure in violence, but I don't shrink from it either, if I decide it's necessary. I didn't see you holding back when we were fighting for our lives in Morgan's factory."

"That was different!"

"No, it wasn't. We're fighting a war here in the Northside, against some of the most evil and corrupt sons of bitches this city has produced, and we're losing. For every villain we put away, there are ten more queuing up to take his place. The only satisfaction we get out of this job is knowing that things would be even worse without us. Now, am I going to have any more problems with you?"

"No," said Burns. "You've made yourself very clear."

"Good. Now help me get these two bravos inside before they freeze their nuts off."

It didn't take long to discover that none of the distributors knew anything about Morgan's super-chacal. The word from every one of them was that Morgan had gone to ground after his release from custody, and no one had heard anything about him since. Hawk gave them all his best, menacing glare, but they stuck to their story, so in the end Hawk decided he believed them. Hawk and Burns stood together in the street outside the last distributor's warehouse, and looked at each other thoughtfully.

"Maybe Morgan's set up his own distribution network," said Burns.

"No," said Hawk. "If he had, I'd have heard about it."

"You didn't know about the super-chacal."

"That was different."

"How?"

"The drug could be produced and guarded by relatively few people, hidden away in the pocket dimension. A new distribution system would need a lot of people, and some-one would have been bound to talk. No, Morgan has to be using an established distributor. Maybe someone who doesn't normally move drugs, but has the right kind of contacts."

"Maybe." Burns pulled his cloak tightly about him, and stamped his feet in the snow. "So, what's our next step?"

"We go and talk with the one man who might know what Morgan is up to; the man who knows everything that's going on in the Northside, because nothing happens here without his approval. The big man himself: Saint Christophe."

Burns looked at him sharply. "Wait a minute, Hawk, even I've heard of Saint Christophe. He takes a cut from every crime committed in Haven. Word is he has a dozen judges in his pocket, and as many Councillors. Not to mention a personal army of four hundred men, and a private mansion better protected than Guard Headquarters. We don't stand a chance of getting in to see him, and even if we did somehow manage it, he'd probably just have us killed on sight. Slowly and very horribly."

"Calm down," said Hawk, amused. "We're not going anywhere near his house."

"Thank all the Gods for that."

"I've got a better idea."

Burns looked at him suspiciously. "If it involves bursting in on him where he works and smashing up his desk, you are on your own. Saint Christophe is the only person in the Northside with an even worse reputation than you."

"Have you finished?" said Hawk.

"Depends," said Burns darkly. "Tell me your idea."

"Every day, at the same time, Saint Christophe has a bath and sauna at a private little place not far from here. It's pretty well-guarded, but there's a way to get in that not many people know about. I did the owner a favour once."

"And at what time of day does Saint Christophe visit this bathhouse?" said Burns.

"About now."

Burns nodded glumly. "I thought so. You've had this in mind all along, haven't you?"

Hawk grinned. "Stick with me, Burns. I know what I'm doing."

Burns just looked at him.

The private baths turned out to be a discreet little place tucked away on a side street in a surprisingly quiet and upmarket area right on the edge of the Northside. It stayed quiet and upmarket because the Northside's more successful villains used the area for their own rest and relaxation, and everyone else had the sense to stay out of their way. Everyone except Hawk.

He walked breezily down an alleyway and slipped into the baths through a door marked "Staff Only." Burns hurried in after him and shut the door quickly behind them, his heart beating uncomfortably fast. Hawk looked around once to get his bearings, then set off confidently through a maze of corridors that Burns wouldn't have tackled without a map and a compass. Every now and again they encountered a member of the staff, but Hawk just nodded to each attendant briskly, as though he had every right to be there, and the attendant just nodded back and continued on his way. Burns grew increasingly nervous, and felt a growing need to find a privy.

"Are you sure you know where you're going?" he whispered harshly.

"You must learn to trust me, Burns," said Hawk airily. "The owner himself showed me this route. We'll find Saint Christophe in cubicle seventeen, just down this corridor here. Assuming he hasn't changed his routine."

"And if he has?"

"Then we'll just walk up and down the corridor, slamming doors open, till we find him."

Burns realised with a sinking heart that Hawk wasn't joking. He thought about the number of major villains who were probably relaxing all unknowing behind the other doors, and swallowed hard. He started to plot an emergency escape route back through the corridors, realised he was hopelessly lost, and felt even worse.

Cubicle seventeen looked like all the others, a plain wooden door with a gold filigree number. Hawk put his ear against the door and listened for a moment, then stood back and loosened the axe at his side. Then he kicked the door open, strolled casually into the steam-filled sauna and leaned against the door, holding it open. Burns stood in the doorway, keeping one eye on the corridor, in case some of the staff happened along. The steam quickly cleared as the temperature dropped, revealing Saint Christophe sitting at the back of the room, surrounded by twelve muscular female bodyguards wearing nothing but sword belts.

The bodyguards surged to their feet, grabbing for their swords as they recognised the Guards' uniforms. Hawk just leaned against the door, and nodded casually to Saint Christophe. Burns wanted desperately to draw his sword, but had enough sense to know it wouldn't help him much if he did. His only hope was to brazen it out and hope Hawk knew what he was doing. He squared his shoulders and lifted his chin, and gave the bodyguards his best intimidating glare. If it bothered them at all, they did a great job of hiding it. And then Saint Christophe stirred on his wooden bench, and everybody's attention went to him. He gestured briefly to his bodyguards, and they all immediately put away their swords and sat down again, ignoring the two Guards. Burns blinked. He couldn't have been more surprised if they'd all started speaking in tongues.

Saint Christophe was a big man, in more ways than one. Though no longer personally involved in any particular racket, every other villain in the city payed him homage, not to mention tribute. He funded a great many operations, and planned many more, but never took a single risk himself. He ran his organization with brutal efficiency and was reputed to be one of the richest men in Haven, if not the Low Kingdoms. He had a partner, once. No one knew what happened to him. It wasn't considered prudent to ask.

The man himself was over six feet tall, and was reputed to weigh three hundred and fifty pounds. Sitting down, he looked almost as wide as he was tall, a mountain of gleaming white flesh running with perspiration. Rumor had it there was a surprising ammount of muscle under all the fat, and Burns believed it. Even sitting still, Saint Christophe exuded an air of overwhelming menace—partly from his imposing bulk, and partly from his unwavering, lizardlike gaze. His face was blank and almost childlike, his features stretched smooth like a baby's by his fat, an impression heightened by his thin, wispy hair. He moved slightly, and the wooden bench groaned under his weight. His bodyguards were already beginning to shiver from the dropping temperature, but he didn't seem to notice it. His gaze was fixed entirely on Hawk, ignoring Burns, for which Burns was very grateful. When Saint Christophe finally spoke, his voice was deep and cultured.

"Well, Captain Hawk. An unexpected pleasure. It's not often you come to see me."

"I have a problem," said Hawk.

"Yes, I know. You have a talent for annoying important people, Captain, but this time you have surpassed yourself. The Guard wants you suspended, a gang from the Devil's Hook has declared vendetta against you, and Morgan wants your head on a platter. You've had a busy morning."

"It's not over yet. I need to know how Morgan is going to distribute his new drug."

"And so you came to me for help. How touching. Why should I help you, Captain Hawk? It would make much more sense to have you killed, here and now. After all, you've caused me much distress in the past. You've shut down my operations, arrested and killed my men, and cost me a great deal of money. I really don't know why I didn't order your death long ago."

Hawk grinned. "Because you couldn't be one hundred per cent sure they'd do the job. And you know that if they didn't kill me, I'd kill them, and then I'd come after you. And all the bodyguards in Haven couldn't keep you alive if I wanted your head."

Saint Christophe nodded slowly, his face impassive. "You always were a vindictive man, Captain. But one day you'll push me too far, and then we'll see how good you really are with that axe. In the meantime, my offer to you still stands. Leave the Guard, and work for me. Be my man. I could make you rich and powerful beyond your wildest dreams."

"I'm my own man," said Hawk. "And there isn't enough money in Haven to make me work for you. You deal in other people's suffering, and the blood won't wash off your money, no matter how many times you launder it through legitimate businesses."

"Anyone would think you didn't like me," said Saint Christophe. "Why should I help you, Captain? You spurn my friendship, throw my more-than-generous offers back in my face, and insult me in front of my people. What is it to me if Morgan is pushing a new drug? If it wasn't him, it would be somebody else. The market's appetite is always bigger than we can satisfy."

"This drug is different," said Hawk flatly. "It turns its users into maddened, unstoppable killers. A few hours after the drug hits the streets, there'll be hundreds of homicidal maniacs running loose in the city. The death toll could easily run into thousands. You can't sell your precious services to dead people, Christophe. You need me to stop Morgan because he threatens your markets. All of them. It's as simple as that."

"Perhaps." Saint Christophe leaned forward slightly, and his wooden bench groaned loudly. His bodyguards tensed for a moment, and then relaxed. "This is important to you, isn't it, Captain?"

"Of course. It's my job."

"No, this is more than just your job; it's become personal to you. One should never get personally involved in business, Captain; it distorts a man's judgement and makes him . . . vulnerable. Let us make a deal, you and I. You want something from me, and I want something from you. I will agree to shut down all distribution networks in Haven for forty-eight hours. More then enough time for you to find Morgan and put a stop to his plans. In return . . . you will leave the Guard and work for me. A simple exchange, Captain Hawk. Take it or leave it."

"No deal," said Hawk.

"Think about it, Captain. Think of the thousands who'll die if you don't find Morgan in time. And you won't, without my help. You really don't have a choice."

"Wrong. You're the one who doesn't have a choice." Hawk fixed Saint Christophe with his cold glare, and the bodyguards stirred restlessly. "The Guard still has some of the super-chacal we confiscated from Morgan's factory. Whoever made the drug disappear from Headquarters missed one batch. So either you co-operate, and tell me what I need to know, or I'll see that when the drug finally gets loose, you'll personally get a good strong dose. If Haven's going to be torn apart because of you, I'll see you go down with it."

"You wouldn't do that," said Saint Christophe.

"Try me," said Hawk.

For a long moment, nobody spoke. The atmosphere in the sauna grew dangerously tense. Burns glanced from Hawk to Saint Christophe and back again, but neither of them looked to be giving way. He let his hand drift a little closer to his sword. All it would take was one sign from Saint Christophe, and the twelve bodyguards would attack. Hawk might actually be able to handle six-to-one odds with that bloody axe of his, but Burns had no false illusions about his own fighting skills. Maybe, if he was quick enough, he could jump back and slam the door in their faces, slow them down enough for him to make a run for it. That would mean abandoning Hawk . . .

"Very well," said Saint Christophe. "I agree. I will see to it that the distribution networks are shut down for twenty-four hours."

"You said forty-eight," said Hawk.

"That was a different deal. You have twenty-four hours, Captain. I suggest you make good use of them, since regretfully I have no idea as to where Morgan might be at present. He seems to have disappeared into a hole and pulled it in after him. But Captain, when this is over, you will answer to me for your threats and defiance. Please close the door on your way out."

Hawk turned and left without speaking. Burns hurried after him, shut the cubicle door firmly, and then ran after his partner as he strode off down the corridor.

"I don't believe what I just saw," said Burns in amazement. "You faced down Saint Christophe without even drawing your axe, and got him to agree to help the Guard. That's like standing in the harbour and watching the tides go out backwards."

Hawk shrugged. "It was in his interests to help, and he knew it."

"Where did you find the extra batch of super-chacal? I thought it had all disappeared."

"It did. I was bluffing." Burns looked at him speechlessly. Hawk grinned. "There's more to surviving in the Northside than knowing how to use an axe."

Hawk was never sure how he knew when he was being followed, but over the years he'd learned to trust his instincts. He glanced at Burns, but he was apparently lost in his own thoughts and hadn't noticed anything. Hawk slowed his pace a little, and found various convincing reasons to look innocently around him. He frowned as he spotted not one tail but several, moving casually through the crowd after him and Burns. Whoever they were, they must be pretty good to have got so close without his noticing them before. His frown deepened as he realised the tails were gradually moving so as to surround him and Burns. It was looking more and more like an ambush, and they'd chosen a good spot for it. The street was growing increasingly narrow, and was blocked off at both ends by market stalls. There were alleyways leading off to both sides, but none of them seemed to lead anywhere helpful. And the next main intersection was too far away, if it came to running. Besides, Hawk didn't believe in running. He let his hand fall casually to the axe at his side, and looked for the best place to make a stand.

"I make it seven," said Burns quietly. "They picked us up not long after we left the baths."

"I wasn't sure you'd even noticed we were being followed."

"Working in the Westside, I spent a lot of time escorting gold- and silversmiths to the banks with their week's receipts. There's nothing like guarding large ammounts of money in public to make you aware of when you're being followed. So what are we going to do? Make a stand?"

"I don't think we've much choice. And it's eight, not seven. See that man in the doorway, just ahead, pretending not to watch us?"

"Yes. Damn. And if we can see eight, you can bet there are just as many more lurking somewhere handy out of sight, just in case they're needed. I don't like the odds, Hawk."

"I've faced worse."

"I wish you'd stop saying that. It's very irritating, and I don't believe it for a moment. Who do you think they are? Morgan's people?"

"Seems likely. He must have known I'd have to go to Saint Christophe eventually, so he just staked the place out and waited for us to turn up. Damn. I hate being predictable."

"We could go back to Saint Christophe and ask for protection."

"You have got to be joking. He'd love that. Besides, I have my reputation to think of."

"If wc don't think of something fast, you're going to be the most reputable corpse in the Northside!"

"Calm down, Burns. You worry too much. If the fighting ground is unfavourable, then the obvious thing to do is change the fighting ground. You see that fire-escape stairway, to your right?"

"Yeah, what about it? Hey, wait a minute, Hawk. You can't be serious . . ."

"Shut up and run."

Hawk sprinted forward, with Burns only a pace or two behind. Their followers hesitated a moment, and then charged after them, forcing their way through the crowd with brutal efficiency. Hawk reached the metal stairway, and ran up it without slowing, taking the steps two at a time. Burns hurried after him, the fire escape shuddering under their combined weight. Hawk pulled himself up onto the roof and scurried across the uneven tilework to crouch beside the nearest chimney. Burns clattered unsteadily across to join him, and clutched at the chimney stack to steady himself. Hawk shot him a grin.

"Check the other side of the roof; see if there's any other way to get up here. I'll prepare a few nasty surprises."

"You're just loving this, aren't you?" said Burns through clenched teeth, hugging tight to the chimney.

"What's the matter with you?"

"I hate heights!"

"Oh, stop complaining, and get over to the other side. This is the perfect spot to take them on; lots of hiding places, and they're just as much at a disadvantage as we are. Trust me, I've done this before."

Burns scowled at him, reluctantly let go of the chimney, and moved cautiously across the tiles towards the spine of the roof. "All right, what's the plan, then?"

"Plan? What do we need a plan for? Just find something to hide behind, and jump out on anything that moves!"

Burns disappeared over the roof ridge, muttering to himself. Hawk looked quickly about him, taking in the gables, cornices, and chimney stacks that jutted from the undulating sea of roofs to cither side. He drew his axe and waited patiently in the shadows of the chimney, listening for the first giveaway sound. It was at times like this that he wished he carried a length of tripwire.

He looked around him, taking in the state of the roof. A lot of snow had fallen away from the tiles, pulled loose by its own weight and the vibrations of passing traffic below, but there was enough left to make the tiles suitably treacherous. A sudden thud followed by muffled curses from the other side of the roof suggested that Burns had reached the same conclusion. Hawk grinned suddenly, as an idea hit him. He moved carefully away from the chimney, unbuttoned his fly and urinated over a stretch of apparently safe tilework. It steamed on the air, but froze almost as soon as it spread out across the tiles. Hawk finished and quickly buttoned up again, wincing at the cold. He looked round sharply as he caught the muffled sound of boots treading quietly on the metal stairway, and he scurried back to crouch down on the opposite side of the chimney stack. He breathed through his nose so that his steaming breath wouldn't give him away, and clutched his axe firmly.

He listened carefully as the first man stepped off the stairway onto the roof, hesitated, and then moved slowly forward. Timing his move precisely, Hawk suddenly emerged from behind the chimney, swinging his axe in both hands. Morgan's man spun round just in time to receive the heavy axehead in his shoulder. The blade sheared clean through his collarbone, and blood flew steaming on the bitter air. The impact drove the man to his knees. Hawk pulled the axe free, put a boot against the man's shoulder and pushed. The man-at-arms screamed once as he slid helplessly across the roof and over the side.

Hawk heard footsteps behind him and turned just in time to see the second man hit the patch of frozen urine. The swordsman's feet shot out from under him and he all but flew off the edge of the roof. The third man was standing by the fire escape with his mouth hanging open. Hawk bent down, snatched up a handful of snow, and threw it at him. As the man-at-arms raised his hand instinctively to guard his face, Hawk stepped carefully forward and swung his axe in a vicious sideways arc. The axehead punched clean through the man's rib cage and sent him flying backwards. He disappeared over the edge of the roof and fell back down the fire escape. There was a brief flurry of yells and curses from the other men coming up the stairway, and Hawk grinned. He hurried forward, and his feet shot out from under him.

He hit the roof hard, and slid kicking and cursing towards the edge of the roof. He threw aside his axe and grabbed at the iron guttering as he shot past it. He got a firm grip on the trough with both hands, and the sudden shock of stopping almost wrenched his arms from his sockets. The guttering groaned loudly, but supported his weight. Hawk hung there for a moment, breathing hard, his feet dangling above the street far below, and then he started to pull himself back up. The trough groaned again and shifted suddenly. There was a muffled pop as a rivet tore free, and Hawk froze where he was. The guttering didn't look at all secure, especially when seen from underneath, and he didn't think it would hold his weight much longer. On the other hand, one sudden movement might be all it would take to pull it away completely. He pulled himself up slowly and carefully, an inch at a time, ignoring the sudden groans and stirrings from the ironwork, and swung one leg up over onto the roof. A few moments later he was back on the roof, reaching for his axe and wiping sweat from his forehead. The sound of approaching feet on the fire escape caught his attention again and he grinned suddenly as a new idea came to him.

He moved carefully over to the metal stairway and looked down. Seven men-at-arms were heading up towards him. They looked grim, and very competent. Hawk waved at them cheerfully, and then bent forward and stuck his axehead between the side of the stairway and the wall. He threw his weight against the axe, and the fire escape tore away from the wall with almost casual ease. The seven swordsmen screamed all the way down to the street below. Hawk put his axe away. Sometimes there was a lot to be said for cheap building practices.

He clambered up to the roof ridge and looked down the other side. Burns was crouching at the edge of the roof, sword in hand, keeping watch from behind a jutting gable. There was no sign of any more men-at-arms. Hawk called out to Burns, and he jumped half out of his skin. He spun round, sword at the ready, and then glared balefully as he saw it was only Hawk.

"Don't do that!"

"Sorry," said Hawk. "I take it none of the men-at-arms got this far?"

"Haven't seen hide nor hair of them. I don't think they were interested in me, only you. How many came after you?"

"Ten," said Hawk, casually.

"Bloody hell. What happened to them?"

Hawk grinned. "We had a falling out."

They made their way back to Headquarters, but though there were no further incidents, Hawk couldn't shake the feeling they were still being followed. He tried all the usual tricks to make a tail reveal himself, but he didn't see anyone, no matter how carefully he checked. It was always possible his current situation had him jumping at shadows, but he didn't think so. The crawling itch between his shoulder blades stayed with him all the way back to Guard Headquarters. He stopped at the main doors and peered wistfully down the street at The Cloudy Morning tavern. A drink would really hit the spot now, after the long day's exertions, but he could just visualize the look on Burns's face if he were to suggest it. All the partners he could have chosen, and he had to pick a saint in training. He strode scowling into Headquarters, and everyone hurried to get out of his way. Burns walked silently beside him, nodding casually to familiar faces. He'd been unusually quiet ever since Morgan's people jumped them. Hawk shrugged mentally. Apparently Burns was still mad at him for not trying to bring in his attackers alive. As if he'd had a choice, with ten-to-one odds.

They made their way through the building, going from department to department, ostensibly just passing the time of day with their co-workers, but always managing to slip in the occasional probing question. It was hard going. None of the Guards wanted to talk about Morgan or his drugs, and in particular no one wanted to be seen talking to Hawk.

Overnight he'd become bad news, and no one wanted to get
too close in case some of the guilt rubbed off on them. The
sudden reticence was unnerving. Usually Headquarters was
buzzing with gossip about everything under the sun, most
of it unprovable and nearly all of it acrimonious, but now all
Hawk had to do was stick his head round a door and silence
would fall across the room. Hawk gritted his teeth and kept
smiling. He didn't want anyone to think the silence was
getting to him. And slowly, very slowly, he started getting
answers. They were mostly evasive, and always hushed, but
they often told as much by what they didn't say as what they
did. And the picture that gradually emerged was more than
a little disturbing.

Mistress Melanie of the Wardrobe department didn't know
anything about Morgan or the missing drugs, but she did let
slip that the campaign of silence was semiofficial in origin.
Word had come down from Above that the Morgan case was
closed. Permanently. Which suggested that someone High
Up was involved, as well as someone at Headquarters. That
was unusual; corruption in the higher ranks of the Guard
tended to be political rather than criminal. A clerk in Intelligence quietly intimated that at least one Guard Captain
was involved. And a pretty well-regarded Captain, too. He
wouldn't even hint at a name.

Hawk and Burns hung around the Constables' cloakroom
for a while, but it soon became clear that the Constables
were uneasy in their company and had nothing to say. The
Forensic Laboratory was up to its eyes in work, as usual,
and the technicians were all too busy to talk. Vice, Forgery,
and Confidence Tricks were all evasive and occasionally
openly obstructive. Hawk had his enemies in the Guard,
and some saw this as their chance to attack while he was
vulnerable. Hawk just kept on smiling, and made a note of
certain names for later.

Of all the departments, the Murder Squad turned out to be
the most forthcoming—probably because no one was going
to tell any of its members who they could and couldn't talk
to. They were the toughest of the tough, took no nonsense
from anyone, and didn't care who knew it. Unfortunately,

what they knew wasn't really worth the telling. The crates of super-chacal had been taken down to the storage cellars, and signed in, all according to procedure. But when the time came to check the contents, there was no sign of the crates anywhere. Everyone in Stores swore blind that no one could have got to the drugs without breaking Stores' security, and all the wards and protections were still in place, undisturbed. Which meant it had to be an inside job. Someone in Stores had been got at. But when the Stores personnel were tested under truthspell, they all came out clean as a whistle. So whoever took the drugs had to be someone fairly high up in the Guard, with access to the right keys and passwords. Hawk mentioned the possibility of a Captain on the take. There was a lot of shrugging and sideways glances, but no one would admit to knowing anything definite. Hawk thanked them for their time, and left.

That just left the Drug Squad, but as Hawk expected, no one there would talk to him. They were already under suspicion themselves, and weren't about to make things worse by helping a pariah like Hawk. He nodded politely to the silent room, and then he and Burns left to do some hard thinking. They found an empty office, barricaded the door to keep out unwelcome visitors, and sat down with their feet propped up on either side of the desk.

"The more I learn, the less this case makes sense," said Hawk disgustedly. "There's no way anyone could have got those crates out of Stores without somebody noticing, passwords or no passwords. I mean, you'd have needed at least half a dozen people just to shift that many crates. Someone in Stores has got to be lying."

"But they all passed the truthspell."

"That doesn't necessarily mean anything. It's possible to beat the truthspell, if you know what you're doing."

"It could have been sorcery of some kind," said Burns. "Morgan had one sorcerer working for him in that factory; who's to say he doesn't have another one working for him?"

"Could be," said Hawk. "Hell, I don't know. I don't know anything anymore. Did you see their faces in the Drug Squad? I know those people. I've worked with practically everyone in that room at one time or another, and they looked at me like I was a stranger. It was the same with all the others; they don't trust me anymore, and the fact of the matter is, I don't trust them either. I don't know who to trust anymore. You heard what Intelligence said; it isn't just a Captain who's on the take, it's a well-respected Captain. There aren't too many of those."

"Maybe we should go talk to Commander Glen."

"No. I don't think so."

Burns looked at him. "Are you saying you don't trust Glen either? He's the one who gave you this brief, told you to find out what's going on!"

"He's also the one who let Morgan go. And it's clear there's been a lot of pressure coming down from Above to keep people quiet. What better way to conceal a potentially embarrassing investigation than to be the one who set it up?"

"But why would someone like Glen bother about a few missing drugs?"

"He wouldn't. More and more it seems to me the drugs are only a part of this. Something else is going on, something so big they can't afford for it to come to light."

"They?" said Burns.

Hawk shrugged. "Who knows how far up the corruption goes? Why stop at a Captain or a Commander? Morgan said there was a lot of money to be made out of this super-chacal. Millions of ducats. And don't forget, most of the top people in the Guard are political appointees, and there's a damn sight more corruption in politics than there ever was in the Guard."

"Hawk," said Burns carefully, "this is starting to sound very paranoid. We're going to need an awful lot of hard evidence if we're to convince anyone else."

"We can't go to anyone else. We're all alone now. We can't trust anyone—not our colleagues, not our superiors, not our friends. Anyone could be working for the other side." Hawk hesitated, and looked intently at Burns. "You know, you don't have to stay with me on this. When I asked you to be my partner, I didn't know what we were getting into. There's still time for you to get out, if you want. Things could get very nasty very quickly once I start pushing this."

Burns smiled. "You're not getting rid of me that easily. Especially not now the case is getting so interesting. I'm not convinced about this massive conspiracy of yours, but there's no doubt something fascinating is going on. I'm with you all the way, until we break the case or it breaks us. Morgan's people killed my partner. I can't turn my back on that. So, what's our next step?"

"There's only one place we can go," said Hawk slowly. "The Guard Advisory Council."

Burns gaped at him for a moment. "You've got to be kidding! They're just a bunch of businessmen, Guard retirees and idealistic Quality who like to see themselves as a buffer between the Guard and the Council's politics. They mean well, but they're about as much use as a chocolate teapot. I mean, they're very free with their advice, but they don't have any real power. They're mostly just public relations. How can they help us?"

"They're all people in a position to have a finger on the pulse of what's happening in Haven. And just maybe they're divorced enough from both Guard and Council not to be tainted by the present corruption. Maybe we can get some answers there we won't get anywhere else. It's worth a try."

"Yes, I suppose it is." Burns hesitated a moment. "Hawk, this Captain who's working for Morgan. What if it turns out to be someone we know? Maybe even a friend?"

"We do whatever's necessary," said Hawk flatly. "Whoever it is."

Burns looked as though he was going to say something more, and then both he and Hawk jumped as someone knocked briskly on the office door. They both took their feet off the desk, and glanced at each other.

"Captain Hawk?" said a voice from outside. "I have a message for you."

"How did he know where to find me?" said Hawk quietly. "No one's supposed to know where we are."

"What do we do?" said Burns.

"Answer him, I suppose." Hawk got up and walked over to the barricaded door. "What do you want?"

"Captain Hawk? I have a message for you, sir. I'm supposed to deliver it in person."

Hawk hesitated, and then shrugged. He pulled away the chairs holding the door shut, drew his axe, and opened the door. A Guard Constable looked at him, and the axe, and nodded respectfully.

"Sorry to disturb you, Captain. It's about the child you rescued from under the collapsed tenement. The little girl."

"I remember her," said Hawk. "Has there been some improvement in her condition?"

"I'm sorry, sir. She's dead. I'm told she never regained consciousness."

"I see. Thank you." The Constable nodded and walked away. Hawk closed the door. "Damn. Oh damn."

Out in the corridor, the Constable smiled to himself. The news had obviously shaken Hawk badly. And anything that slowed Hawk down had to be good for Morgan and his backers. The Constable strode off down the corridor, patting the full purse at his belt and whistling cheerfully.

5

Under Siege

Fisher peered out the study window, chewing thoughtfully on a chicken leg she'd liberated from the delegates' lunch
time snack after they'd disappeared back into the pocket
dimension. She'd spent the last half hour checking out the
house security and searching for weak spots, but she had
to admit ap Owen seemed to know what he was doing.
Every door and window had locks or bolts or both, and
they were all securely fastened. There were men-at-arms
in servants' livery on every floor, making their rounds at
random intervals so as not to fall into a predictable routine.
Routines could be taken advantage of. There were caches
of weapons stashed all over the house, carefully out of
sight but still ready to hand in an emergency. Outside, the
grounds were a security man's dream. All the approaches
were wide open—nowhere for anyone to hide—and the
thick covering of snow made the lawns impossible to cross
without leaving obvious tracks.

All in all, everything was calm and peaceful, and showed
every sign of staying that way. Which was probably why
Fisher was so bored. Ap Owen's people seemed to regard
her as an outsider, and her appointment as some kind of
negative appraisal of their own abilities. As a result, none
of them were talking to her. Ap Owen himself seemed
friendly enough, but it was clear he was the worrying

type, constantly on the move, checking that everything was running smoothly. Fisher wandered aimlessly around for a while, committing the layout of the house to memory and trying to get the feel of the place.

It was an old house, creaking and groaning under the weight of the winter cold, with a somewhat erratic design. There were rooms within rooms and corridors that led nowhere, and shadows in unexpected places. But everything that could be done to make the house secure had been done, and Fisher couldn't fault ap Owen's work. She should have felt entirely safe and protected, and it came as something of a surprise to her to find that she didn't. Deep down inside, where her instincts lived, she couldn't shake off the feeling she—and everyone else in the house—was in danger. No doubt part of that uneasiness came from knowing there was a pocket dimension nearby. After what had happened in the Hook she was more than a little leery of such magic, for all of ap Owen's reassurances. But more than that, she had a strong feeling of being watched, of being under siege. She had only to look out of a window to feel the pressure of unseen watching eyes, as though somewhere outside a cold professional gaze was studying her dispassionately, and considering options.

And so she'd ended up back in the study, staring out the wide window at the bare, innocent lawns and wondering if she was finally getting paranoid. Ap Owen acted as if he was expecting an attack at any moment, and she was beginning to understand why. There was a definite feeling of anticipation in the air, of something irrevocable edging closer; as though her instincts were trying to warn her of something her mind hadn't noticed yet. She threw aside her chicken leg, turned her back on the window defiantly, and looked around for something to distract her. Unfortunately, the study was briskly austere, with the bare minimum of chairs and a plain writing table. Bookshelves lined two of the walls, but their leather-bound volumes had a no-nonsense, businesslike look to them. There was one portrait, on the wall behind the desk, its subject a straight-backed, grim-faced man who apparently hadn't approved of such frivolities as having your portrait painted. The study had clearly been intended as a room for working, not relaxing.

Fisher leafed through some of the papers on the desk, but ap Owen's handwriting was so bad they might have been written in code for all she could tell. She looked thoughtfully at the wine decanters left over from the delegates' break, and then looked away. She'd been drinking too much of late. So had Hawk. Haven did that to you.

There was a definite crawling on the back of Fisher's neck, and she strode back to the window and glared out at the featureless scene again. The snow-covered lawns stretched away before her, vast and unmarked. There were no trees or hedges, nothing to hide behind. Everything was quiet. Fisher yawned suddenly, and didn't bother to cover her mouth. She'd been hoping to snatch a couple of hours' sleep here, but it seemed her nerves were determined to keep her restless and alert. She almost wished that someone would attack, just to get it over with.

She started to turn away from the window, and then stopped, startled, and looked quickly back again. The wide open lawns were empty and undisturbed; no one was there. But for a moment she could have sworn . . . It came again, a sudden movement tugging at the edge of her vision. She looked quickly back and forth, and pounded her fist on the windowsill in frustration. There couldn't be anyone out there. Even if they were invisible, they'd still leave tracks in the snow. Things moved at the corner of her eyes, teasing her with glimpses of shapes and movement that refused to come clear. She backed slowly away from the window and drew her sword. Something was happening out there. There was a sound behind her and she spun round, dropping into a fighter's crouch. Ap Owen raised an eyebrow, and she flushed angrily as she straightened up.

"Dammit, don't do that! Come and take a look, ap Owen. Something's going on outside."

"I know. Half my people are giving themselves eyestrain trying to get a clear look at it."

"Do you know what it is?"

"I have a very nasty suspicion," said ap Owen, moving over to join her before the window. "I think there's someone out there, hiding behind an illusion spell. It must be pretty powerful to hide his trail as well, but as he gets closer to the house the protective wards are interfering with the spell, giving us glimpses of what it's hiding."

"You think it's just one man?"

"Not really, no. Just wishful thinking. I've put my people on full alert, just in case."

"Does whoever's out there know we've spotted something?"

"Beats me. But they haven't tried anything yet, which suggests they still trust in the illusion to hide their true strength."

Fisher scowled out the window, and hefted her sword restlessly. "All right, what do we do?"

"Wait for them to come to us. Let's see if they can even get in here before we start panicking. After all, it would need a bloody army to take this house by force."

There was a sudden, vertiginous snap and the world jerked sideways and back again, as the house's wards finally broke down the illusion spell and showed what lay behind it. The wide lawns were covered with armed men, and more were pouring through the open gates. Dressed in nondescript furs and leathers, they advanced on the house in a calm, professional way. Fisher swore respectfully. There had to be at least two hundred men out there.

The four marble statues had come alive, and were cutting a bloody path through the invaders. They were coldly efficient and totally unstoppable, but were hard put to make any impression on so many invaders. Half a dozen guard dogs blinked in and out of existence as they threw themselves at the intruders, leaping and snapping and now and again tearing at a man on the ground, but again there were simply too few of them to make any real difference. No one had expected or planned for an invasion on such a scale as this.

"I don't want to disillusion you, ap Owen," said Fisher grimly, "but it looks to me like they've got a bloody army. We are in serious trouble."

"You could well be right. From the look of them, they're mercenaries." He yelled something out the study door, and four footmen burst in, each carrying a longbow and a quiver of arrows. Ap Owen grinned at Fisher. "They don't have much use for bows in the Guard, but I've always believed in them. You can do a lot of damage with a few bowmen who know what they're doing."

"No argument from me," said Fisher. "I've seen what longbows can do."

The footmen set up before the window, pulling off their long frock coats to give them more freedom of movement. Fisher and ap Owen struggled with the bolts that held the window shut, until Fisher lost her temper and smashed the glass with the hilt of her sword. Ap Owen threw the window open and stepped back to let the archers take up their position. Bitter cold streamed in from outside, and the archers narrowed their eyes against the glare of the snow. The attacking force realised the grounds were no longer hidden behind the illusion spell, and ran towards the house, howling a dissonant mixture of war cries and chants. Sunlight flashed on swords and axes and morningstars. Fisher couldn't even guess how many attackers there were anymore. The archers drew back and released their bowstrings in a single fluid movement, and four of the attackers were thrown backwards with arrows jutting from their bodies. Their blood was vividly red on the snow. The archers let fly again and again, punching holes in the attacking force, but they just kept coming, ignoring their dead and wounded.

"They're professionals, all right," said ap Owen calmly. "Mercenaries. Could be working for any number of people. Whoever it is must want us shut down really badly. An army that size doesn't come cheap. I didn't think there were that many mercenaries for hire left in Haven."

"How long before reinforcements can get here?" said Fisher tightly.

"There aren't going to be any," said ap Owen. "We're on our own. Low profile, remember? Officially, no one knows we're here."

"And we're expendable," said Fisher.

"Right. We either win this one ourselves, or we don't win it at all. What's the matter, don't you like a challenge?"

Fisher growled something under her breath. The first handful of mercenaries to reach the window ducked under the flight of arrows and clambered up onto the windowsill. The archers threw aside their bows and grabbed for their swords. Fisher thought briefly of the door behind her. She didn't believe in suicide missions. On the other hand, she didn't believe in running, either. She moved quickly forward to join ap Owen and the archers, and together they threw the first mercenaries back in a flurry of blood and gore. More of the attackers crowded in to take their place. The war cries and chants were almost deafening at close range. Fisher glanced at ap Owen, saw him palm a pill from a small bottle, and swallow it. He caught her gaze and smiled.

"Just a little something, to give me an edge. Want one?"

"No thanks. I was born with an edge."

"Suit yourself. Here they come again." He breathed deeply as the drug hit him, and smiled widely at the mercenaries. "Come and get it, you lousy bastards! Come one, come all!"

The main bulk of the attack force hit the window like a breaking wave, and forced the archers back by sheer force of numbers. Fisher was swept aside, fighting desperately against a forest of waving blades. In moments the room was full of mercenaries, most of whom ran past the small knot of beleaguered defenders and on into the house. Fisher and ap Owen ended up fighting back to back, carving bloody gaps in the shifting press of bodies. The archers fell one by one, and Fisher and ap Owen were slowly driven back across the room, away from the window, as more mercenaries poured in. There seemed no end to them.

Ap Owen laughed happily and mocked his opponents as he fought, and none of the mercenaries could get anywhere near him in his euphoric state. Fisher fought doggedly on. Mercenaries fell dead and dying around her, their blood staining the expensive carpet. Her footing became uncertain as bodies cluttered the floor, and it was getting harder to find room to swing her sword. She yelled at ap Owen to get his attention.

"We've got to get out of here, while we still can!"

"Right!" yelled ap Owen, grinning widely as he slit a mercenary's throat. "Follow me!"

They made a break for the door, ploughing through the startled mercenaries, and cutting down anyone who got in their way. They burst out into the hall, and Fisher was surprised to find it deserted. Ap Owen headed for the stairs, with Fisher close behind.

"They don't know where the Talks are really being held, so they're wasting time searching the house," said ap Owen breathlessly, as he took the steps two at a time. "But I know where there's an emergency entrance into the pocket dimension. We can hide out in there till the fighting's over."

"What about your people?" protested Fisher angrily. "You can't just abandon them!"

"They know where the entrance is, too. If they've got any sense, most of them are probably already there."

Fisher heard boots hammering on the stairs behind her, and threw herself forward. The mercenary's sword swept past her head, the wind of its passing tugging at her hair. Fisher kicked backwards, and the swordsman's breath caught in his throat as the heel of her boot thudded solidly into his groin. Fisher turned around to finish him off, and found herself facing a dozen more mercenaries charging up the stairs towards her. She put a hand on the groaning swordsman's face and pushed him sharply backwards. He fell back down the stairs and crashed into his fellows, bringing them all to an abrupt halt. Fisher smiled angelically at the chaos, and turned her back on them. Ap Owen was nowhere to be seen.

She swore harshly, and hurried up the stairs to the landing. She paused at the top of the stairs to get her bearings, and an axe buried itself in the wall beside her. She ran along the hallway, glaring about her. Ap Owen couldn't have gone far. If he had, she was in trouble. He'd never got around to telling her where the doorway to the pocket dimension was. Sounds of hot pursuit grew louder behind her, and from all around came shouts and curses and war cries as the invaders spilled through the house, searching for the Peace Talks.

A mercenary burst out of a door just ahead of her, and Fisher ran him through while he was still gaping at her. She jerked the sword free and then had to back quickly away as two more men charged out of the room at her.

She put her back against the railing that ran the length of the hall and swung her sword in wide arcs to keep them at bay. Two-to-one odds didn't normally bother her, but this time she was facing two hardened professionals in very cramped surroundings, with nowhere to retreat and no one to guard her blind sides. It was at times like this that she realised how much she missed Hawk. She cut viciously at one mercenary's face, and he stepped back instinctively. Fisher darted for the gap that opened up, but the other swordsman was already there, forcing her back with a flurry of blows. Fisher fought on, but she could feel her chances of getting out alive slipping away like sand between her fingers.

And then one of the mercenaries went down in a flurry of blood, and ap Owen was standing over him, flashing his lunatic grin. Fisher quickly finished off the other mercenary, and the two Guards sprinted down the hallway, with more mercenaries in hot pursuit.

"Where the hell have you been?" demanded Fisher. "I turned my back on you for a moment and you were gone!"

"Sorry," said ap Owen breezily. "I didn't notice you weren't still with me. Now save your breath for running. We've got a way to go yet, and those bastards behind us are getting closer."

A mercenary appeared out of nowhere before them and ap Owen cut him down with a single slash. Fisher hurdled the writhing body without slowing, and followed ap Owen up a winding stairway. Footsteps hammered on the steps behind her, and she glanced back over her shoulder to see half a dozen mercenaries charging up the stairs after her. Fisher looked away and forced herself to run faster. She was already bone-tired after the long day, and her legs felt like lead, but somehow she forced out a little extra speed. Ap Owen, of course, was running well and strongly, buoyed up by his battle drug. Sweat ran down Fisher's face, stinging her eyes, and her sides ached as her lungs protested. She just hoped she wouldn't get a stitch. That would make it a perfect bloody day.

Ap Owen led her down a wide corridor at a pace she was hard pressed to match, but somehow she kept up with him. The growing crowd of mercenaries snapping at her heels helped. It worried her that she hadn't seen any of ap Owen's men. Surely some of them should have got this far. . . . A growing suspicion took root in her that they were all dead. That all the house's defenders were dead, apart from her and ap Owen. Which made it all the more urgent they reach the pocket dimension and warn the delegates.

Ap Owen darted suddenly sideways through an open doorway, and Fisher threw herself in after him. She whirled to slam the door shut, but three mercenaries forced their way in. Fisher cut down one with a single, economical stroke, and his blood flew on the air, but another swordsman darted in under her reach and cut at her leg. Her thick leather boot took most of the impact, but she could still feel blood trickling down her leg inside the boot. She drove the man back with a frenzied attack, and for a moment held off both opponents by the sheer fury of her attack. And then ap Owen was with her, cutting and hacking like a madman, and between them they finished off the mercenaries, slammed the door shut, and bolted it. It rattled angrily in its frame as men on the other side put their shoulders to it.

The two Guards stood exhausted over the bodies for a moment, breathing harshly, and then ap Owen jerked his thumb over his shoulder. "Let's go. The doorway's here."

Fisher looked behind her, and saw an open door hanging unsupported in the air. Beyond the door there was only darkness. "About time. I just hope the pocket dimension turns out to be a damn sight more secure than this house."

"It is; I guarantee it. Now let's move it, please."

He grabbed her arm and hauled her through the doorway. The door slammed shut behind them, and disappeared from the room. There was a brief sensation of falling, and then Fisher was in the Peace Talks' hidden room. The delegates rose startled from their seats around a long table, staring at her and ap Owen. She quickly put up a hand to forestall their questions.

"The house is overrun with mercenaries. We had to cut and run. No choice. How many more of our people made it here?" She took in their blank faces, and looked away. "Damn. Then I think it's fair to assume they won't be coming. We're the only survivors."

She looked quickly round the sparsely furnished, medium-sized room, and then blinked as she found there was no sign of the doorway. All four walls were blank. She shrugged, and looked at ap Owen, who was sitting on the floor beside her with his head hanging down. He was deathly pale, with sweat streaming off his face, and obviously using all his willpower to keep from vomiting. Fisher smiled sourly. That was battle drugs for you. Great as long as adrenalin kept you going, but once you stopped there was hell to pay. She manhandled him onto a chair, and then turned back to the delegates. They were obviously waiting for a more detailed report, and it was clear from their faces that their patience had just about run out. Really, the report should come from ap Owen, as the senior Captain in charge of security, but since he was out of it and likely to stay that way for some time . . . Fisher realised she was still holding her sword, and sheathed it. She drew herself up to parade rest, thought briefly about saluting the delegates, and then decided the hell with it.

"We're in trouble," she said bluntly. "Someone hired a small army of mercenaries, backed them up with some heavy-duty sorcery, and sent them here looking for you. Our security forces didn't stand a chance; the mercenaries rolled right over us. Unless some more of our people arrive in the next few minutes, you'd better get used to the idea that your entire security force now consists of ap Owen and me. And there aren't going to be any reinforcements. We're trapped in here, and the house is crawling with mercenaries."

"It's not quite as bad as you make it sound, Captain," said Lord Regis calmly. "Firstly, we are quite safe here. The dimensional doorways won't open to the mercenaries, and the only other way in is to open a new doorway. Even a high-level sorcerer couldn't do that without first knowing the exact co-ordinates of this dimension, and those are, of course, only known to a select few. All we have to do is sit tight and wait for the mercenaries to leave. They won't hang around once they realise we're not in the house; an attack like this is bound to have been noticed, especially in Low Tory. I think we can be fairly confident that the Guard is on its way here even as we speak."

"Wait a minute," said Fisher. "How will we know when it's safe to leave?"

Lord Regis shrugged. "We'll just stick our heads out from time to time, and see what's happening."

Ap Owen chuckled harshly. "He means you and I will stick our heads out, Fisher. They're not going to take any risks. Right, my lord?"

"Of course," said Lord Regis. "That is what you're here for, isn't it?"

Fisher looked at ap Owen. His face was still pale, but he was sitting up straight and he looked a lot more composed. "How are you feeling?"

"Great. The side effects don't last long."

"Long enough to get you killed, if they hit you at the wrong moment."

Ap Owen shrugged.

"You're all missing the point," said Major de Tournay. "How did the mercenaries know to look for us here? Our location was supposed to be secret."

"He has a point," said Lord Regis, looking heavily at ap Owen.

The senior Captain nodded unhappily. "Somebody must have talked. Someone always talks, eventually. But since they couldn't know about this dimension, it doesn't really matter. The mercenaries will just ransack the house, find no trace of the Talks, and report back to their masters that you weren't here. They'll be called off, and you can resume the

Talks undisturbed, secure in the knowledge they won't be back again. And if the Guard reacts fast enough, they might even be able to follow the mercenaries back to their masters, and we can round them all up in one go."

"Excellent!" said Lord Nightingale. "This might turn out to have been all for the best, after all."

"Hold it just a minute," said Fisher, and there was a harshness in her voice that drew all eyes to her. "A lot of good men died out there, trying to protect you and your precious Talks. Doesn't that mean anything to you?"

The two merchants, Rook and Gardener, had the grace to look a little embarrassed. The two Majors stirred uncomfortably, but said nothing. Lord Regis looked thoughtfully at the floor. Lord Nightingale sniffed.

"They were just doing their job," he said flatly. "They understood they were expendable. As are we all."

"I'm sure that'll be a great comfort to their widows," said Fisher. "Those men never stood a chance, thanks to your insistence on low profile security."

"That's enough, Captain!" said Lord Regis sharply. "It's not your place to criticise your superiors. We have to consider the bigger picture."

Fisher gave him a hard look, and then turned away. Ap Owen relaxed slightly, and felt his heart start beating again. He didn't think Fisher would actually punch out a lord, but you could never tell with Fisher.

"His lordship is right, Fisher," he said carefully. "The safety of the delegates must come first. That's what they told us when we took on this job, remember? Now take it easy. We're all perfectly safe in here; nothing can reach us."

He broke off suddenly, as far away in the distance a bell tolled mournfully. The sound seemed to echo on and on, faint but distinct, as though it had travelled impossible distances to reach them. They all stood silently, listening. The bell tolled again and again, growing slowly louder and more mournful, like the bell from a forgotten church deep in the gulfs of hell. Fisher's breathing quickened, and her hand fell to her sword. Something was out there in the dark, she could feel it; something awful. The pealing of the bell grew louder still, painfully loud, until everyone in the hidden room had their hands pressed to their ears. And then the air split open above them, and nightmares spewed out into the waking world.

Creatures with insane shapes that hurt and disturbed the human eye fought and oozed and squirmed out of nowhere, and fell writhing to the floor. There were things with splintered bones and snapping mouths, and nauseating shapes that twisted through strange dimensions as they moved. Creatures with flails and barbs and elongating limbs. A monstrous slug with grinding teeth in its belly fell heavily onto the conference table, its weight cracking the thick wood from end to end. A clump of ropy crimson intestines squeezed out of the split in the air, and dropped squirming to the floor, where it dripped acid, eating holes in the carpet. The conference room rang to a cacophony of screams and howls and roars, drowning out the madly tolling bell.

For a moment everyone froze where they were, and then Fisher threw herself forward, swinging her sword in wide, vicious arcs. Strangely colored blood flew steaming on the air as her blade sank deep into unnatural flesh, and howling shapes rose up in fury all around her. Ap Owen was quickly at her side, and together they forced the demons back. Major Comber and Major de Tournay drew their swords and fought back to back, old enmities forgotten in the face of a common foe. They cut and thrust with professional efficiency, and nothing could stand against them for long.

The two traders, Rook and Gardener, retreated into a corner and defended themselves with unfamiliar swords as best they could. Creatures swarmed eagerly about them, scenting easy prey. Lord Regis fought stubbornly with his back to a wall, barely keeping the fangs and claws from his throat but determined not to give in. Lord Nightingale cleared a space around him with inspired swordsmanship, chanting all the while in a harsh forced rhythm. Human blood flowed as the creatures pressed closer, forcing their way past flashing steel by sheer force of numbers. And still more shapes poured through the split in the air, and there seemed no end to them.

"We've got to get out of here!" Fisher yelled to ap Owen.

"We can't," he answered, grunting with the effort of his blows. "Only Regis and Nightingale can open the door. And they both look a bit busy at the moment. See if you can work towards them, take some of the pressure off."

Fisher tried, but the growing tide of creatures forced her back foot by foot, and ap Owen had to struggle to keep his place at her side. A jagged cut on his forehead leaked blood steadily down one side of his face, and he had to keep blinking his eye to clear it. A raking claw suddenly opened up a long, curving gash across Fisher's hip and stomach, and she stumbled and almost fell as the pain flared through her. Ap Owen darted in to try and cover her, and a long, serrated tentacle whipped around his shoulders and snatched him up into the air. Fisher hacked at the tentacle, but it wouldn't let him go. Comber and de Tournay were soaked with blood from a dozen minor wounds, but were still holding their ground and grimly defying the creatures to move them. Rook and Gardener had already fallen and disappeared beneath a heaving throng of frenzied shapes. Lord Regis was struggling, tears of exhaustion running down his cheeks, but Lord Nightingale ignored him, concentrating on his rhythmic chanting.

And then Nightingale's voice rose sharply to a shout, and the split in the air slammed together and was gone. The creatures burst into flames, screaming and thrashing as a searing golden fire consumed them, leaving nothing but ash. The faraway bell was quiet, and the only sound in the hidden room was the harsh breathing and groans of the two Guards and the surviving delegates.

Fisher sat with her back braced against a wall, watching exhaustedly as ap Owen slowly picked himself up from where the burning tentacle had dropped him. The two Majors leaned on each other, exchanging quiet compliments. Lord Regis bent wearily over two bodies lying twisted and still in a corner, then straightened up and turned away. Rook and Gardener were beyond help. Regis looked across at Lord Nightingale, calmly cleaning the blood from his sword in the middle of the room.

"I didn't know you were a sorcerer, Nightingale."

The Outremer lord shrugged easily. "I'm not, really. I just like to dabble."

"Still, I would have expected you to mention it," said Regis. "Since one of the conditions for these Talks was that none of the delegates be a sorcerer."

"I told you," said Nightingale. "I'm not a sorcerer. Just a gifted amateur."

"That's not the point. . . ."

"Can we discuss this later?" said Fisher sharply. "We need a doctor in here."

"I'm afraid that's out of the question," said Nightingale. "We're under orders not to reveal our presence. Officially, no one is to know we're here."

"You have got to be joking," said Fisher. "If there's one thing we can be certain about, it's that our enemies know where we are. Both the mercenaries and those stinking creatures knew exactly how best to catch us off guard. Somebody's talked. We're not a secret anymore. So forget the low profile nonsense, and get some real protection in here. We were lucky this time. We won't be again. And get me a bloody doctor, dammit! If this wound gets infected, I'll sue."

Some time later, after a number of hasty but effective healing spells, Fisher and ap Owen made their rounds of the house, looking over their new, improved security force and checking the faces of the dead mercenaries before they were carried out. None of the mercenaries had been taken alive. Those who hadn't managed to escape before Guard reinforcements arrived killed themselves rather than be captured.

"Which suggests to me they were under a geas," said ap Owen. "It had to be some kind of magical compulsion. Mercenaries don't believe in that kind of loyalty to a cause.

Any cause. We fight strictly for cash; nothing else. I had wondered if I might know any of these poor bastards, but I don't recognise any faces. Probably hired outside Haven, to prevent any rumours of the attack from getting out. You couldn't hope to hire this many men in Haven and keep it quiet."

"Right," said Fisher. "Somebody always talks. Which brings us back to the attack on the pocket dimension. Someone betrayed us. But who knew?"

"Not many. The delegates, you and I and the ten Guards working inside the house, and Commander Glen, of course." He stopped suddenly, and he and Fisher looked at each other. "Glen?" said ap Owen finally.

"Why not?" said Fisher. "He's the only one who had nothing to risk by talking."

Ap Owen shook his head firmly. "Glen's a hard bastard, but he's no traitor. Much more likely one of my people talked to the wrong person before they came here, and that person sold us out."

Fisher nodded unhappily. She couldn't ask any of ap Owen's people about it; none of them had survived the mercenaries' attack.

"That's not our only problem," said ap Owen dourly. "Nightingale's knowledge of magic has got everyone worked up. Admittedly he saved all our arses when the creatures broke through, but now Regis and Major Comber are worried sick he could be using his magic to influence their minds during the Talks. But they accepted him as a delegate and if they reject him now, Outremer will undoubtably retaliate in kind, and what progress they have achieved so far will all have been for nothing. So, for the moment the Talks are officially in abeyance until Rook and Gardener can be replaced. And you can bet Haven's replacement will know some sorcery, just to be on the safe side."

Fisher growled something unpleasant, and then shrugged. "At least the Talks will continue. That's something."

"Until the next attack."

"You think there'll be another one?"

"Bound to be. Too many interests want these Talks to fail. And we're stuck right in the middle. And I thought being a Guard would be a nice cushy number after being a mercenary. . . ."

6

Naming the Traitor

"This is where the Guard Advisory Council meets? I've seen more impressive outhouses." Hawk shook his head disgustedly. "Maybe you were right after all, Burns. Anyone who has to meet in a dump like this isn't going to be in any position to help us."

Burns kept a diplomatic silence, but his shrug spoke volumes. Hawk glared at the building before him, and wondered if there was any point in going inside. The Guard Advisory Council held its meetings in a rented room over a corner grocer's shop; the kind that stays open all hours and sells anything and everything. The two-storey building was fairly well-preserved, but looked like it hadn't seen a coat of paint in generations. Hawk peered into the shop through the single, smeared window, and one glance at the interior was enough to convince him he'd have to be bloody hungry before he ate anything that came from this grocer. He could practically see plague and food poisoning hiding in the shadows and giggling together. And he didn't want to think about what the unfamiliar cut of meat optimistically labelled "Special Offer" might be. He turned away and looked around the street. Passersby kept their heads down to avoid his gaze and hurried by the two Guards, trying hard to look innocent and failing miserably. Mostly they just succeeded in looking furtive. It was that kind of neighbourhood.

"I did try to tell you, Hawk," Burns said finally. "These people are Advisors, and that's all. They have no real power or influence, even if they like to think they have. They come up with the odd good idea on occasion, and they're good public relations, so the Guard tolerates them, but that's as far as it goes."

"Maybe," said Hawk. "But none of that's important. What matters is that these people are connected to the Guard, but not a part of it. They ought to know some of what's going on but still be distanced enough that they can talk to us without fear of retribution. Dammit, Burns, I need someone to talk to me. I need information. We're flailing about in the dark and getting nowhere, and Morgan's sitting out there somewhere safe and secure, laughing at us. We need a lead, something to point us in the right direction at least."

"And you think we're going to get that from the Guard Advisory Council?"

"It's worth a try, dammit! We've got to do something!"

He strode angrily forward, ignored the shop doorway and stomped up the iron fire escape that clung uncertainly to the side of the building. Burns followed him silently. His partner was getting desperate, and it was beginning to show. Hawk stopped before the plain wooden door at the top of the fire escape, and banged loudly on it with his fist. Someone inside pulled back a sliding panel and studied Hawk for a long moment. Then the panel slid shut and there was the sound of bolts being drawn back. The door swung open, and Hawk and Burns stepped inside. The door closed quickly behind them.

The rented room turned out to be surprisingly cosy. Oil lamps shed a golden glow over the wood-panelled walls and chunky furniture, and large, comfortable-looking chairs had been set out before a crackling fire. Two men stood together by the chairs, facing Hawk and Burns with determined casualness. They looked embarrassed, and perhaps just a little frightened. Hawk studied them both, letting the silent moment stretch uncomfortably. Burns stirred at his side, but made no move to intervene. The man to their left coughed nervously.

"Good evening, Captains. It's good of you to visit us. It's not often the Guard takes an interest in our work. I'm Nicholas Linden, the lawyer. Perhaps you've heard of me. . . . And this is my associate, Michael Shire, once a Captain in the Guard, now retired."

Hawk nodded politely. Burns had already filled him in on who he'd be meeting, and he had no trouble recognising these two from Burns's descriptions. Nicholas Linden was tall and fashionably slender, with watchful eyes and a practiced smile. He'd started out as a meat-wagon chaser specialising in insurance cases, and had graduated through a series of well-publicized cases and well-bribed juries to a fairly successful practice in Low Tory. At which point he suddenly developed a civic conscience, and started agitating to put an end to the kind of sharp practices that had got him where he was. His fellow lawyers had persuaded him to join the Guard Advisory Council, in the hope of distracting him from things best left alone. To no one's surprise, it worked.

Michael Shire had been a Captain in the Guard for twenty years, before taking early retirement to go into business for himself as a private security consultant. He'd done well for himself over the past few years, and was now responsible for most of the hired muscle in the Westside. He was a large, squarish man in his late forties, wearing fashionably garish clothes that didn't suit him. He had a calm, self-satisfied face, with cold, expressionless eyes.

And these were two of the people who'd set themselves up as the Guard's conscience.

"Will any of the others be joining us?" Hawk said finally, his voice flat and cold.

"I'm afraid not, Captain," said Linden, perhaps just a little too quickly. "You must understand, we all lead very busy lives outside the Advisory Council, and it isn't always possible for all of us to attend meetings called at such short notice. However, your message did say your business was both urgent and important, so Michael and I agreed to . . .

represent the others. Do please sit down, Captains. And help yourselves to some wine, if you will."

Hawk shook his head shortly, and sat down. Burns also declined the wine, and he and the Advisors joined Hawk in the chairs before the fire. Linden and Shire looked at Hawk and Burns expectantly. Hawk set out the situation as clearly and concisely as he could, taking it from the raid on Morgan's factory to his growing belief that Morgan must be bribing someone fairly high up in the Guard. There was a pause, and then Shire snorted loudly.

"Don't see what all the fuss is about," he said gruffly, meeting Hawk's gaze unflinchingly. "There's always been a certain amount of . . . private enterprise in the Guard. It's only natural for Guards to augment their income on occasion, given the low wages. Everyone takes a special payment now and again; it's a sort of unofficial tax. If people want real protection, they've got to be prepared to pay for it. After all, a contented Guard is much more likely to look out for you, isn't he? I think you're taking this too seriously, Captain Hawk."

"I'm not talking about half-arsed protection rackets," said Hawk. "I'm talking about a high-ranking Guard who's been bought and paid for by one of the city's biggest drug barons."

"So what?" said Shire flatly. "This is Haven, remember? There are people here it doesn't pay to cross, and Morgan is very definitely one of them. It's not in the Guard's interest to start a war it couldn't win."

"This time it's different," snapped Hawk. "Morgan's new drug is too dangerous to be ignored. And whoever's helping him in the Guard is putting the whole damned city at risk, just to carn himself a nice little bonus. This isn't just corruption anymore; it's treason. I want this bastard, and you're going to help me identify him. You're both in a position to hear things, know things; people will talk to you who wouldn't talk to me. I want to know what they've been saying. I want the name."

Shire and Linden glanced at each other, and then Linden leaned forward. He fixed Hawk with an earnest gaze, and chose his words carefully. "You must understand, Captain, that my associate and I are taking a not inconsiderable risk in seeing you at all. You've made yourself dangerous to know. You've been making enemies, the wrong sort of enemies. The word is that Morgan has important friends, very well-connected people, who aren't taking kindly to your enquiries. Anyone who openly helped you would be putting his own neck in the noose."

"Refusing to talk to me can be pretty risky too," said Hawk calmly. "I'm not playing by the rules anymore. I don't have the time."

Shire sniffed. "Threats won't get you anywhere. To put it bluntly, Morgan is connected to people who are scarier than you'll ever be."

"Then why are you talking to us at all?" asked Burns.

"Because I was a Captain in the Guard for twenty years . . ." said Shire slowly, " . . . and there are some things I won't stand for. I might have taken the odd gratuity in my time, and looked the other way when I was told, but I was always my own man. No one tells me to roll over on my back and play dead, like a good dog. Not then or now. Linden came to see me earlier today. He was scared. He overheard something he shouldn't have, from one of Morgan's people, and he knew he wouldn't be safe as long as he was the only one who knew it. So he told me, and now he's going to tell you. There's no doubt that Morgan, or the people he's associated with, have infiltrated the Guard at practically every level. From the bottom right to the top. But for once, we have a name. Morgan's bought himself a Guard Captain, someone so loyal and honourable as to be above suspicion."

"Tell me the name," said Hawk.

Linden swallowed hard, and looked briefly at Shire for support. "You're not going to like this, Hawk. I don't have any proof or evidence; this is just what I heard. I could be wrong."

"Just tell me the bloody name!"

"Fisher," said Linden. "Captain Isobel Fisher."

Hawk launched himself out of his chair, both hands reaching for Linden. Burns grabbed at him, but Hawk shook him off. He took two handfuls of Linden's shirt and lifted him up into the air. The lawyer's face lost all its color, and his mouth worked soundlessly. Shire and Burns pulled at Hawk's arms, but he ignored them, thrusting his face close to Linden's.

"You're lying, you bastard. They put you up to this, didn't they? Didn't they! Tell me the name, you bastard. Tell me the real name!"

Linden struggled to get his breath, his eyes wide and staring. "Please . . . please don't hurt me. I'm sorry. . . ."

"He's telling the truth," said Shire urgently, almost shouting in Hawk's ear to get his attention. "Let him go, Hawk. He's just telling you what he heard."

"That's right," said Burns. "Let him go, Hawk. Come on, let him go."

Hawk dropped the lawyer back onto his chair, and turned away, breathing heavily. Linden clawed at his collar, trying to get some air into his lungs. Burns and Shire backed away from Hawk, watching him carefully.

"Take it easy, Hawk," said Burns soothingly. "It's just hearsay, that's all. They said themselves they had no proof or evidence."

"It's a lie," said Hawk.

"Of course it is."

"Don't use that tone of voice with me, Burns! I'm not a child. I'm not a fool, either. This is just something Morgan's come up with to try and slow me down, distract me from going after him. Well, it's not going to work. I know Isobel. It's impossible that she could be involved in anything like that. She wouldn't . . ."

"Of course not," said Burns. "Let's go, Hawk. We've got what we came for."

Hawk nodded, and headed for the door without even looking at Shire and Linden. Burns made a quick, placating gesture to them, and hurried out after his partner.

Down in the street, Hawk strode blindly through the snow and slush, staring straight ahead. People took one look at his face and hurried to get out of his way. Burns walked along beside him, studying his partner anxiously.

"We have to talk about this, Hawk," he said finally. "Of course the idea of Fisher being a rogue is ridiculous, but we can't just ignore it, either. Whoever the corrupt Captain is, it has to be someone who'd normally be above suspicion. Someone so honest and trustworthy no one would ever connect them with Morgan. Everyone we've talked to agrees on that, and it has to be said there aren't many Captains in the Guard who fill that description."

"It isn't Isobel," said Hawk.

"Then why name her in front of someone like Linden? Even if Morgan's people knew they were being overheard, how would they know you'd end up talking to Linden? You only decided to visit the Advisors a short time ago."

"He would have passed the word on, and it would have got round to me eventually. It's just a distraction, that's all."

"Sure," said Burns. "Look, whoever the rogue is, it has to be someone close to us. Close to you. Someone who knows you well enough to know the people you'd go to for answers. How else did Morgan's people know where to ambush us after we left Saint Christophe?"

"We're probably being watched," said Hawk.

"Not all the time; we'd notice."

"Well, maybe he's got a sorcerer watching us magically! He had a sorcerer at the factory; how do we know he hasn't got another magic-user working for him?"

"I think we'd better leave this till later," said Burns suddenly, his voice low. "We're being followed again. Look around you."

Hawk's preoccupation fell away in a moment, and he looked casually about him, his hand moving naturally to the axe at his side. "Hell's teeth, how did I miss them? They're not exactly professional quality, are they? That's what happens when you let yourself get distracted. There's a lot of them; I make it twenty-seven, most of them wearing gang colors. How about you?"

"I only see twenty-two, but I'll take your word for it. They must have known we were going to be here, Hawk;

it's another bloody ambush. Better thought-out than the last one, too; they're all around us this time."

Hawk sniffed. "It doesn't matter. I'm just in the mood to cut up a few bad guys."

Burns looked at him sharply. "Wait a minute, Hawk; this is no time to start feeling heroic. We're outnumbered more than ten to one here."

"So what do you suggest? Put up our hands and surrender nicely, and hope we'll get taken as prisoners of war? This may be a war, Burns, but no one's taking any prisoners."

"We could always make a run for it."

"We could, but how far do you think we'd get? The streets are narrow and crowded, and we're both dog-tired while our pursuers look decidedly fresh. There aren't even any fire escapes in easy reach this time. They've planned this well, Burns, and we walked right into it."

The street grew increasingly quiet as they strode along, and passersby began moving into the shelter of doorways so as to be safely out of the way when the killing began. Everyone knew what was happening. The ambushers weren't even trying to hide themselves anymore.

Hawk stopped walking and looked openly around. Burns stopped beside him, and looked quickly about for any escape route he might have missed. The ambushers were everywhere, moving confidently forward. Now that they were all out in the open, Burns counted twenty-nine of them. They were dressed in ragged furs and leathers, and carrying clubs and swords and axes. Some had broken bottles and lengths of metal piping. They all looked lean and hungry and very dangerous. Burns looked to Hawk for support, and a sudden chill ran through him. Hawk was smiling, a cold and nasty death's-head grin. Burns felt an instinctive need to back away. He'd seen his partner go through many moods that day, but this was something new and awful, and for the first time Burns understood why Hawk was so widely feared in the Northside. At this moment, he looked vicious and deadly and totally unstoppable.

Burns made some kind of noise in his throat, and Hawk looked at him briefly. "These aren't Morgan's people," he said, his voice eerily calm and even. "These are street-gang toughs from the Devil's Hook. I beat up their leader, a piece of slime called Hammer, earlier on this morning. He must have declared vendetta on me. Knew I should have killed him."

He fell silent as one of the ambushers stepped forward, but his death's-head grin never wavered. He recognised the man as the gang leader, and drew his axe with a flourish. Hammer stopped where he was and called out to Hawk, his voice carefully loud and mocking.

"I've been looking for you, Hawk. No one messes with me and gets away with it, not even the high and mighty Captain Hawk. Don't look so tough now, do you? Now you're on your own and I've got my people here to back me up. You're going to die slow, Hawk. We're all going to take turns cutting on you; going to take our time and get real inventive. You're going to scream and cry and beg for death before we're through."

Hawk laughed at him, and there was enough naked violence in the sound to silence the gang leader almost in mid-word. The watching ambushers stirred uneasily. Hawk swept his axe back and forth before him. "Who's first?" he said mockingly. No one moved. Hawk glanced at Burns. "Get out of here while you can," he said quietly, his voice calm and conversational. "They don't care about you; they just want me. If you make a run for it, they'll probably let you go."

"Forget it," said Burns. "They'll kill me anyway, just for being a Guard, and being with you. Believe me, if I could see a way out of this mess, I'd take it. I'm not crazy. Do me a favour, Hawk: Next time you feel like punching out a gang leader, don't do it in front of witnesses. All right, you're supposed to be the expert on winning against impossible odds: What are we going to do? There's nowhere to run, and if we try and make a stand they'll roll right over us."

Hawk nodded, still grinning at the ambushers and hefting his axe. Burns looked away. The grin was starting to unnerve him. One of the toughs stepped forward. Hawk looked at him, and the tough stopped where he was.

"I think our best bet is to try and lose them in the side streets and alleyways," said Hawk calmly. "They're narrow and crowded, and the gang will only be able to come at us a few at a time. We should be able to take them easily, as long as we keep our heads."

"What if they've staked out the alleyways with more of their people?" said Burns tightly.

"Then we fight our way through and keep running. Maybe we can outrun them."

"What happens if we get trapped in a dead end?"

"Then we see how many of the bastards we can take with us. Think positive, Burns. We're not dead yet, and I've faced worse odds in my time."

"When?" demanded Burns. Hawk just grinned at him.

Hammer suddenly barked an order, and the toughs moved forward from every direction. Hawk lifted his axe threateningly and then sprinted towards the nearest side street. Burns charged after him, his stomach churning sickly. Three gang members made to block their way. Hawk cut down the first two with vicious sweeps of his axe, and hit the third man with a lowered shoulder. The massive tough was thrown aside like a child, and Burns hacked halfway through his waist without even slowing. He pounded after Hawk down the narrow street, with the gang howling behind them.

More gang members appeared out of darkened alley mouths, but somehow Hawk and Burns managed to cut a way through them and keep on running, leaving bodies lying in pools of vivid scarlet on the grimy snow. Hawk glared about him, trying to figure out exactly where he was. This wasn't an area he knew particularly well and he couldn't afford to stop and look for landmarks hidden or disguised by the recent snow. His breath burned in his chest, and he could feel the beginnings of a stitch in his side. Normally he prided himself on his stamina, but it had been a long day and it wasn't getting any shorter. From the sound of it, Burns was finding the going equally hard.

And then they rounded a sharp corner and skidded to a halt as they saw more gang members waiting for them.

There were ten of them blocking the narrow alley, all armed with some kind of weapon and smiling confidently. Hawk glanced back over his shoulder. The pursuers were coming up fast, and there was no way out. Hawk felt more anger than anything. Being killed in a gang ambush was such a stupid way to go. And now he'd never get the chance to clear Fisher's name. He'd make them pay for that. He threw himself at the smiling faces before him, and laughed aloud as he saw their expressions change to shock and terror as his axe tore through them like firewood. He sensed Burns fighting desperately at his side, but Hawk had no room in him for anything but rage.

The first few died easily before his fury, but there were too many of them for him to break through, and soon the rest of the gang arrived. Hawk and Burns fought back to back, surrounded by screaming mouths and flailing weapons, hemmed in by the jostling press of bodies. The sheer number of attackers gave Hawk and Burns a fighting chance; the gang were so eager to get at their victims that they kept getting in each other's way and deflecting many of the blows meant for the two Guards. Hawk fought on fiercely, sending blood spraying through the freezing air, but knew it was only a matter of time before someone got in a lucky blow. Then his guard would drop, and he'd go down under a dozen swords. And if he was lucky, he'd die before Hammer could pull his people off. He was just sorry he'd dragged Burns into this. Hawk fought on, as much out of stubbornness as anything. If he had to die, he was going to make them work for it. A sword licked in past his defences, and punched through his side and out again. Blood ran thickly down his hip and leg, and the strength seemed to flow out of him along with the blood. He swung his axe clumsily, and the swords were everywhere.

A thick mist sprang up suddenly in the alleyway, diffusing the amber lamplight in strange ways, and misty grey ropes curled and tightened around the gang members' throats. They dropped their weapons to tear at the strangling mists with desperate hands, and fell gagging to the ground. Curling mists lashed viciously among the gang, sending them flying this way and that, and they fled screaming back down the alley and out into the surrounding streets. The mists flowed after them like a relentless river. Dead bodies littered the alley. Hammer stared uncomprehendingly about him, abandoned by his men, and then backed away as Hawk loomed up before him, grim and bloody, his gaze colder than the winter could ever be. He turned to run, and Hawk cut him down with one blow of his axe. Hammer fell dying to the ground, and there was enough anger still in Hawk for him to regret it was over so quickly.

He turned to see how Burns had fared, and fell back against a wall as the wound in his side caught up with him. The stabbing pain filled his mind, and then a strong arm curled around his shoulders, supporting him, and a cool hand pressed against his bloody side. There was a brief, crawling sensation as the wound knitted itself together, and then the sorceress Mistique stepped back and grinned at him.

"I thought I'd leave the gang leader for you to take care of personally. But I can't believe you just walked right into that ambush. If I hadn't been following you too, they'd have had to bury what was left of you in a closed coffin."

"I had a lot on my mind," said Hawk, feeling gingerly at his side. "And it must be said, this has not been one of my better days. Thanks for the rescue."

"You're welcome. But next time don't go dashing off like that. I nearly didn't catch up in time."

Hawk nodded, and looked across at Burns. The man's clothing was soaked in blood, but he nodded quickly to Hawk and Mistique to show he was all right. Hawk looked down at the gang leader, lying dead and broken on the dirty snow, and swore softly.

"I should have taken him alive. He might have been able to answer some questions."

Burns frowned. "What could he have known? He isn't connected with Morgan; he was just after you because you made him lose face in front of his people."

"Someone had to have told him where to find us! He couldn't have followed us all the way from the Hook."

"He didn't," said Mistique flatly. "I've been following you for some time, and they were already here waiting for you when you went in to talk to the Advisors."

Hawk looked at her narrowly. "I didn't see you following us."

Mistique smiled. "Well, after all, darling, I am a sorceress."

Hawk nodded slowly. "All right; want to tell me why you were following us? And why you dropped out of sight right after we left the Hook?"

The sorceress scowled, and leaned back against the alley wall with her arms folded. "I know something that certain important people don't want known. Something . . . dangerous. So I decided to disappear for a while, and do some hard thinking. I needed someone to talk to, someone I could trust. You were the obvious choice, Hawk, but I had to be sure you were what you were supposed to be. So I've been following you." She looked at him for a long moment. "Even now I'm not sure I'm doing the right thing. You're not going to like this, Hawk."

"Tell me," said Hawk. "Tell me what you know."

"I was talking to one of the prisoners we took in Morgan's factory, before we brought them back to Headquarters," said Mistique steadily. "He was mad as hell because the Guard Captain that Morgan had been paying off hadn't warned them about the raid. I asked him for the Captain's name, but he didn't know it. He knew what the Captain looked like, though. He recognised her when he saw her during the raid.

"It was Fisher, Hawk. Captain Isobel Fisher."

7

Scapegoat

Fisher looked out the repaired study window and glowered sourly at the array of armed men camped out on the wide lawns. There had to be a hundred men out there now, wearing chain mail under their furs and warming their hands at the scattered iron braziers. If the Peace Talks had had this kind of protection before, two of the delegates and all of the original security force might still be alive. Fisher felt obscurely guilty that she hadn't got to know the men under her command before they were killed. As it was, it would take a hell of an army to get past the new security force; that, or a particularly nasty piece of magic. Fisher decided she wasn't going to think about that. She still got edgy every time she remembered the flood of twisted creatures that had come spilling out of the split in reality. She'd only just got over jumping at every sudden noise.

Raised angry voices cut across her reverie, and she turned her back on the window to study the squabbling delegates. Her mouth compressed into a thin, flat line as she realised they were going round and round in the same futile circles. The Peace Talks were becoming increasingly warlike, with the two lords blaming everyone and everything but themselves for the present sorry state of affairs. Lord Nightingale of Outremer was the loudest voice, quite openly determined to lay the blame for everything at Haven's door. Lord Regis was trying to be reasonable and diplomatic, but his temper was visibly shortening, and his voice had already risen to match Nightingale's.

The two Majors, Comber and de Tournay, had withdrawn from the fray and settled themselves in a corner with the drinks cabinet. They were busily comparing whiskies and doing their best to ignore the whole unpleasantness. They had no interest in recriminations or name-calling, and had said so loudly. Unfortunately, it hadn't been loud enough to compete with the racket Regis and Nightingale were making, so their objections had gone completely unnoticed by the two lords.

Captain ap Owen was standing with his back to the fireplace, watching everything and saying nothing. He hadn't spoken a dozen words to anyone since he'd overseen the new security force as they cleared up the mess left by the assault. Fisher understood. The men under his command had been longtime associates and friends, and now he'd lost them all in one brief clash of arms. The bodies were gone now, along with the dead mercenaries, but the smell of blood and death was still strong in the house.

Major Comber stirred suddenly, and slammed the flat of his hand against the top of a nearby table. It made a satisfyingly loud noise, and the two lords shut up and looked round to see what was happening. Comber carefully put down his whisky glass, and glared at each lord in turn.

"I think this nonsense has gone on long enough," he said firmly. "We're supposed to be here to discuss the border problem, not play at who can shout and stamp their foot the loudest. We'll probably never find out exactly who betrayed us, and it doesn't matter worth a damn anyway. The attack was a failure and the Talks can go on. Now, may I respectfully suggest that we get back to what we're supposed to be doing, and leave the squabbling and whining to the politicians. That's what they're paid for."

De Tournay started to nod vigorously in agreement, and then stopped as he realised both Nightingale and Regis were glaring at Comber.

"Your opinion is noted, *Major* Comber," said Lord Regis icily. "But allow me to remind you that your function at these Talks is to provide us with military information and advice. Nothing more. The Lord Nightingale and I are quite capable of deciding what is important here, and right now nothing is more important than determining who betrayed us. We could all have been killed, dammit, and I want to know who was responsible! Particularly since it seems we can't trust our own security people to keep us safe."

He glared at Fisher and ap Owen, who stared back calmly, fully aware that anything they said would only end up being used against them. Major de Tournay stirred in his corner, and then shrugged uncomfortably as Regis turned his glare on him.

"With respect, my lord, no security system is perfect. Fisher and ap Owen did their best, in extremely difficult circumstances."

He shut up as Nightingale turned to glare at him too. Nightingale's voice was low and deadly. "When I want your advice, *Major* de Tournay, I will ask for it. Until then you will oblige me by keeping your mouth shut. Is that clear?"

De Tournay and Comber looked at each other, nodded formally to their respective lords, and returned their attention to the whisky decanters. Regis sniffed, and looked back at Fisher and ap Owen.

"Now then, Captains, it cannot have escaped your attention that our security here has been hopelessly breached. Whether this was the result of internal treachery or simple incompetence on your part has yet to be determined. You can both be very sure there will be a full enquiry into your behaviour today. . . ."

"I don't think we can wait for that," said Nightingale flatly. "Someone has revealed to our enemies not only the location of this house, but also the co-ordinates of the pocket dimension. Quite a few people knew about the house—that was inevitable—but only a handful knew about the pocket dimension. Don't you find it interesting that our security problems only began after Captain Fisher joined us?"

"Oh, come on," said ap Owen immediately. "You're not seriously accusing Fisher? She's a legend in Haven! And she fought like hell against the mercenaries and the creatures in the dimension. In fact, if not for her, I wouldn't have lived long enough to reach the dimension, and you wouldn't have lived long enough to close the dimensional doorway. We owe her our lives!"

"Look at the facts," said Nightingale calmly. "The mercenaries didn't attack the house till she got here, and the creatures didn't attack us until she'd joined us in the pocket dimension. . . ."

"He has a point," said Regis slowly. "And it does seem odd that Captain Fisher should have been in the middle of so much fighting, and come out of it with only minor, superficial wounds."

"She's a good fighter!" said ap Owen. "Everyone knows that."

"No one's that good," said Nightingale.

"And I must admit the new security forces have brought rather disquieting news concerning Fisher's partner, Captain Hawk," said Regis.

"Hawk?" said Fisher sharply. "What about Hawk?"

Regis fixed her with a steady gaze. "It appears that Captain Hawk is completely out of control. He's assaulted a superior officer and gone on a rampage through the city, attacking people in some kind of personal vendetta, and killing anyone who gets in his way. We don't know exactly how many people he's killed, but we have a confirmed account of more than thirty dead, and almost as many injured. At least a dozen were just innocent passersby."

"I don't believe it," said Fisher.

"In view of what you've just told me," said Lord Nightingale, ignoring Fisher, "I don't think I care to trust my well-being to any security force commanded by Captain Fisher. I'm afraid I must insist she be replaced, if the Talks are to continue."

"I have to agree," said Regis. "Well, Fisher, have you anything to say for yourself?"

"I didn't want to come here in the first place," said Fisher. "If you don't want me, I'll leave."

"It's not that simple," said Nightingale coldly. "We can't allow you to just walk out of here. You know too much. And besides, I don't believe in letting traitors walk free. Regis, I want this woman arrested, and held incommunicado till these Talks are over."

Regis nodded. "Fisher, hand over your sword. You're under arrest. The charge is treason."

Nightingale smiled at Fisher coldly. "I'll see you hanged for your part in this, bitch."

Fisher drew her sword and dropped into her fighting stance. "You and what army, Nightingale?"

"Fisher, that's enough!" snapped Regis. "Give your sword to ap Owen. That's an order!"

Fisher laughed at him. "Stuff your order. I may be slow, but I'm not crazy. You're just desperate for a scapegoat, and I look like the best bet. Well, sorry, people, but I'm afraid I must decline the honour."

Regis looked at ap Owen. "Arrest her! Do whatever you have to, but stop her. She mustn't leave here alive!"

Ap Owen hesitated, and Fisher threw a chair at him. She was across the room and out the door before the two Majors could get to their feet and ap Owen could disentangle himself from the chair. Regis and Nightingale remained where they were, shouting orders. Fisher slammed the door shut behind her, grinned briefly as she heard someone crash into it, and then sprinted down the corridor to the front door. She yanked it open and charged out into the grounds. The new security people looked up in surprise, and moved towards her, anticipating some kind of emergency in the house. Fisher grabbed the first officer she saw, and pointed him at the front door.

"Block off that door and don't let anyone out, no matter what! Take as many men as you need. Everything depends on you! Move it!"

The officer threw her a quick salute, and charged towards the door, yelling for his men to follow him. Fisher ran for the front gate, breathlessly informing every man-at-arms she passed of the terrible emergency up at the house. The emergency became more and more terrible, and the details more and more fantastic, as she passed through the main body of men, determined to stir up the maximum confusion. She finally reached the gate, and paused a moment to look back. The men-at-arms were milling aimlessly back and forth, trampling the snow into slush, shouting incoherently to each other, and searching desperately for some sign of the enemy. Fisher grinned, and set off down the street at a fast but eminently respectable pace, so as not to attract too much attention.

First thing was to get rid of the Guard's uniform; it was too distinctive. Maybe change it for a long robe with a hood, something large and bulky enough to substantially alter her appearance. When word finally got out from the house, there were going to be an awful lot of people looking for Captain Fisher. There was no point in trying to protest her innocence. It was clear Nightingale had picked on her as the scapegoat, and the others would go along with him in order to keep the Talks going. As she'd been told from the beginning, the Peace Talks were far more important than any Guard Captain. She was expendable.

But she wasn't about to let anyone or anything get between her and her search for Hawk. From the sound of it, things had got really out of hand since she left him with Burns. She frowned. Strange there hadn't been any mention of Burns. She shook her head fiercely. That could wait. All that mattered was finding Hawk. If he really was out of control, she was the only one with any chance of stopping him. Whatever had happened between Hawk and Morgan, he'd listen to her.

And then they'd work together to find out who the real traitor was. Before, it had just been business. Now, it was personal.

In the study, Lord Regis and Lord Nightingale were taking turns shouting at Captain ap Owen. Outside in the grounds, Major Comber and Major de Tournay were trying desperately to restore some kind of order to the chaos Fisher had made out of the men-at-arms. Half of them were still running around like mad things, looking for something to hit and mistaking each other for the enemy as often as not. Ap Owen listened to the craziness outside, and somehow kept the smile from his lips. Eventually the lords ran out of accusations and curses, and stopped a moment to get their breath back. Ap Owen cleared his throat.

"What exactly do you want me to do, my lords? What are your orders?"

"Find Fisher!" snapped Nightingale, his cheeks mottled with rage. "I don't care how you do it, but find her!"

"Take twenty men and go out into the city," said Regis. "Spread the word among the Guard and on the streets. I'm authorizing you to offer a reward of five thousand ducats for Fisher's capture, dead or alive."

Ap Owen looked at him sharply. "But surely, my lord, we need her alive for questioning?"

"We need her stopped before she can do any more damage," said Nightingale. "As long as she's free, she's a threat. You know her reputation, Captain; if you try and take her alive she'll just kill your men and disappear again. We can't risk that. If you find her, kill her. No quarter, no mercy."

Ap Owen looked at Regis, who nodded steadfastly. "Do whatever you have to, Captain, but don't bring her back alive."

8

Cutting Loose

Burns and Mistique followed Hawk silently as he led the way through a maze of narrow back streets and shadowed alleyways. He'd hardly said a word since Mistique reluctantly named Fisher as the traitor, and his cold, grim visage hadn't encouraged conversation. Burns and Mistique glanced at each other, but a few raised eyebrows and quick shrugs were enough to make it clear neither of them knew what was going through Hawk's mind. Given what he was capable of, his continued silence was worrying. Passersby hurried to get out of his way, but Hawk seemed totally oblivious of everything except his own thoughts. He walked unhurriedly through the shabby streets, staring straight ahead, his bloodied axe still in his hand.

They finally emerged into a quiet side street, and Hawk led his companions into a squalid little tavern called The Dragon's Blood. The air was thick with smoke, and the sawdust on the floor looked like it hadn't been changed in years. Mistique wrinkled her nose. Burns pushed the door closed with his fingertips, and then wiped his hand fastidiously on his cloak. The place was as dark as a coal cellar, with only occasional pools of dirty yellow light at the occupied tables, and two storm lanterns hanging over the bar. The window shutters had been nailed shut to ensure privacy. Shadowed drinkers watched silently as Hawk led his companions to a booth at the back of the room. Conversation slowly resumed as the three Guards seated themselves, but only as a bare murmur. The bartender emerged from behind his bar to serve them personally, and Hawk ordered three beers. They sat in silence until he came back with the drinks. Hawk paid him the exact amount and then dismissed him with a curt wave of his hand. The bartender shrugged, and went back to the bar to continue polishing his glasses with a dirty rag. Mistique looked dubiously at the drink in front of her, and decided that she wasn't thirsty. Hawk took two deep swallows from his beer, and then put the glass down and stared into it.

"The beer's safe enough here," he said quietly, "but don't touch the spirits. Half of it's made from wood alcohol."

Burns sipped at his beer to show willing, and his lips thinned away from his teeth at the bitterness. "Nice place you've chosen, Hawk. Great atmosphere. I'll bet plague rats stay away from here in case they catch something. Do you drink here often?"

"Only when I have some hard thinking to do. No one bothers me here." He drank from his glass again, and Burns and Mistique waited patiently for him to continue. Hawk wiped the froth from his mouth with the back of his hand, and leaned back in his chair, staring out into the gloom around them. "It all comes down to Morgan," he said finally. "He has all the answers. If we're ever going to get to the truth of what's really going on here, we have to find Morgan."

"Half the Guards in Haven are trying to do just that," said Burns. "But Morgan's always been able to disappear when he needed to. He could be anywhere in Haven. Our people are out leaning on every loose mouth in the city, but no one knows anything. Morgan's gone to ground so thoroughly this time that even his own people don't seem to know how to contact him. You must really have thrown a scare into him."

"He can't afford to be totally isolated," said Mistique. "He still has to move his super-chacal before word gets out how dangerous it is. And to do that, he must be doing business, however indirectly, with some distributor."

"Exactly," said Hawk. "Morgan may have crawled into his hole and pulled it in after him, but his lieutenants are still out there, doing business on his behalf. All we have to do is tail them, and eventually one of them will lead us to Morgan."

Burns shook his head. "Hawk, those people are professionals; they'll spot any tail we put on them."

"They won't spot a sorcerer," said Hawk. "How about it, Mistique? Can you follow these people with your magic?"

"There is a way . . . " said Mistique slowly. "But I don't know these lieutenants like you do. You'll have to open your minds so that I can learn what you know. Are you and Burns willing to do that?"

"No," said Burns flatly. "Sorry, Hawk, but there are some things I won't do, for you or anyone else. My thoughts are private, and my memories are my own."

"There's no need to be so defensive," said Mistique. "It's a comman reaction to my ability. Though why anyone should assume their secret thoughts are so fascinating I couldn't resist peeking, is beyond me."

"Take what you need from me," said Hawk. "But don't go wandering. There are things in my mind you don't want to know."

"I can believe that," said Mistique. She closed her eyes, and a cold breeze swept through Hawk's mind, ruffling his thoughts, and picking things up and putting them down again. Images flickered in Hawk's mind like flaring candles, come and gone so quickly he barely recognised them, and then Mistique opened her eyes, and his mind was quiet again. Mistique nodded, satisfied. "Got it. Names and faces for all twenty of his lieutenants. Now I need both of you to sit still and be quiet. This is going to be very difficult, and I can't afford any distractions."

She closed her eyes again and let her mind drift up and out, becoming one with the mists. Wherever mists and fogs rose throughout the city she had eyes and ears. She became the mists, flowing over houses and streets, through keyholes and under doors, and nothing was hidden from her. The mists carried her up into the sky, and she soared high above the city, seeing it spread out below her like a vast dark stone labyrinth of sudden turnings and endless possibilities. Lights burned in its darkness like furnaces in hell. She swooped down over the city, spreading her consciousness among the many streets and alleyways as mists curled everywhere in Haven. Buildings raced past her at bewildering speed, people appearing and disappearing in an instant, but all of them observed and studied and dismissed. Words from a thousand conversations battered her hearing like pounding waves on the rocks outside the harbour. Mistique let it all flow past and over her, sifting through the endless noise and chaos until finally she found what she was looking for.

His name was Griff—a shabby, skinny man with long, greasy dark hair, darting eyes, and a quick, unpleasant smile. He wore a long frock coat mended at the collar and elbows, and carried a quarterstaff. He didn't look like much, but bigger men than he bobbed their heads and smiled nervously in his presence. He was Morgan's eyes and voice and executioner, and everyone knew it. Mistique curled lazily on the air as Griff strode down a gloomy side street, unobtrusively checking now and again that he wasn't being followed. Mistique floated after him, everywhere and nowhere, ahead and behind him.

Griff took a sudden turn into an alleyway and stopped dead, just inside the alley mouth. He looked casually about him to be sure he was unobserved, and then moved slowly forward, counting the steps under his breath. He then stopped, reached out and pressed five bricks in the left-hand wall in a careful sequence. A door slowly appeared in the wall, a great slab of solid steel, featureless save for a single moulded handle, forming itself moment by moment out of the dirty brickwork. Griff waited impatiently, his gaze darting back and forth, and then he pulled the door open, grunting with the effort. A bright crimson light flared out into the alley, and Griff stepped forward into it. The door slammed shut behind him, cutting off the bloody light, and melted back into the brickwork. In the renewed gloom of the alleyway, the roiling mists curled and twisted triumphantly.

In the tavern, Hawk and Burns watched silently as Mistique closed her eyes and fell immediately into a trance state. All trace of personality dropped out of her face as her muscles relaxed completely. The air grew thick and indistinct around her as wisps of mist seeped out of her skin. The mists gradually thickened until they were boiling up off her like ectoplasm at a séance. The tavern quickly emptied as the other customers headed for the door at a run. The bartender disappeared behind his bar. Burns started to rise from his chair, and then sank reluctantly back into it when Hawk glared at him. Hawk watched, fascinated, as Mistique's eyes darted back and forth beneath her closed eyelids as though she were dreaming, and then her eyes snapped open and personality flooded back into her face. The mists in the booth began to dissipate, stirred by a sourceless wind. Mistique fixed Hawk with her gaze.

"I've got him. Morgan's been hiding out in another pocket dimension, hidden off Packet Lane, not ten minutes' walk from here."

"Did you get a look inside?" said Hawk. "Did you see Morgan himself?"

"Not really. I could sense his presence, along with a dozen or so bodyguards, but when I tried to enter I brushed up against another sorcerer's wards, so I got the hell out of there before I gave myself away."

"Are you sure there's just the one sorcerer?" said Hawk.

Burns looked at him. "One is usually enough to screw up any mission."

Hawk ignored him, his gaze fixed on Mistique. "This is the second we've come across already. There might be more."

"No," said Mistique. "There's just the one."

"Good," said Hawk. "Burns and I will take care of the bodyguards. You handle the sorcerer. Only this time, let's all try really hard not to bring the pocket dimension down around our ears. All right?"

• • •

Mistique led the way to Packet Lane, striding confidently through the thickening fog. Hawk carried his axe at the ready and kept a careful watch, but no one seemed to be paying them any particular attention. People tended not to look at Guards if they could help it, on the grounds they didn't want Guards looking at them. Burns grumbled most of the way to Packet Lane, muttering that the odds stank, the whole idea was crazy, and they ought to call Headquarters for a backup. Eventually Hawk said *No* with enough force to prove that he meant it, and Burns shut up and sulked the rest of the way. As long as he did it quietly, Hawk didn't give a damn. He couldn't afford to have Headquarters involved at this stage. If they were, he'd have to tell them about Fisher.

Mistique finally brought them to Packet Lane, and they stood together in the alley mouth, staring into the gloom. Nothing moved in the alleyway, and the shadows lay quiet and undisturbed. Burns drew his sword, and the sudden grating noise was eerily loud on the quiet. He glanced at Hawk, who nodded to Mistique. She walked forward, counting out the steps, and pressed the five bricks in the correct sequence. The huge steel door appeared out of the brickwork, and swung open at Mistique's gesture. They stepped forward into the bright crimson light, and the door swung silently shut behind them.

The three Guards stood close together a moment, squinting into the crimson glare, and then Hawk hissed at Burns and Mistique to spread out. They made too good a target standing as a group. Their eyes quickly adjusted, and Hawk relaxed a little as he realised the long corridor before them was completely empty. The brilliant red light seemed to come from everywhere and nowhere, bathing everything in its bloody glow. The corridor had no furniture, no doors, and no visible turnings off. The walls and the floor were bare wood, not even varnished. Hawk took the point and led the way forward, axe at the ready. Burns and Mistique followed close behind. Their footsteps echoed loudly from the bare wooden floor, no matter how softly they trod.

The corridor seemed to go on forever. Hawk glanced back over his shoulder, and his hackles rose sharply as he saw the corridor stretching away behind him into the distance, with no sign of the door through which they'd entered. He shrugged uncomfortably, and trudged on down the corridor. It had to lead somewhere. The corridor suddenly rounded a corner and branched in two. Hawk looked down both paths, but there was nothing to choose between them. He looked back and forth while Burns and Mistique waited patiently for him to make up his mind, and then he tensed as he heard footsteps approaching. Hawk gestured quickly for the other two to fall back, and they retreated round the corner. Hawk eased back round the corner after them and stood poised, listening to the footsteps draw nearer. A man-at-arms rounded the corner, and Hawk whipped an arm round his throat before he had time to react. The man-at-arms started to call out, and Hawk tightened the hold until all that came out was a strangled croak.

"Don't move," said Hawk quietly. He waited till the man was perfectly still, and then eased his grip a little. The man-at-arms drew in a long, juddering breath. Hawk nodded to Burns, and he stepped forward and took the man's sword. Hawk put his mouth close to his prisoner's ear.

"Morgan. Where is he?"

"Are you crazy? He'll have you killed for this. . . ." He broke off abruptly as the hold round his throat tightened harshly and then relaxed again.

"What's your name?" said Hawk.

"Justin."

"Do you know who I am?"

"No. Who are you?"

"I'm Hawk. Captain Hawk."

"Oh God."

"Where's Morgan?"

"It's not far. I'll lead you to him."

"That's a good boy. I'm going to let you go now. Behave yourself and you might come out of this alive."

He let go of the man-at-arms, and gestured for him to lead the way. Justin nodded jerkily, rubbed at his throat, and set

off round the corner and down the left-hand path. Hawk and
Mistique followed close behind, with Burns bringing up the
rear. Hawk leaned in close to Mistique and spoke softly, so
that only she could hear.

"Is there any way Morgan could know we're coming?
Could his sorcerer have set up any protective wards in
here?"

Mistique shook her head. "If he had, I'd know," she said
softly. "There were wards and magical booby traps crawling
all over the alleyway, but I defused them by summoning the
door correctly. Keep your guard up, though, just in case. If I
were Morgan, I'd have some kind of fall-back defences."

Hawk nodded. "That's probably what the dozen bodyguards are supposed to be. I know how Morgan thinks; I've
met his kind before. He thinks he's so big and powerful
no one would dare just walk in on him. After all, he's got
his own sorcerer and a dozen bodyguards to protect him.
Who'd be crazy enough to come in here after him, in his
own stronghold?"

Mistique looked at Hawk. "He might just have a point."

Hawk smiled. "I've faced worse odds. Morgan's just a
cheap thug with delusions of grandeur. And I'm going to
knock him down and rub his nose in it until he tells me
what I want to know."

The man-at-arms led them through a short series of
passageways to a pair of huge, polished oaken doors.
Somewhere along the way, the sourceless crimson light
had changed to a homely golden glow. There were expensive
paintings and tapestries on the walls, and a deep-pile carpet
on the floor. Hawk looked at the double doors for a long
moment, and then turned and smiled at their guide.

"Well done, Justin. I'm very pleased with you. Mistique,
put him to sleep for a while."

The sorceress locked eyes with Justin, and all the color
drained out of his face. His eyes rolled up in his head and
he fell limply backwards. Burns caught him and lowered
him to the floor. Hawk hefted his axe, breathed deeply, and
then reached forward and carefully opened one of the doors
an inch. He looked back at Burns and Mistique.

"No mercy, no quarter—but whatever happens, I want Morgan alive. He's no use to me dead."

He turned back to the doors, kicked them open, and charged in, axe at the ready. Burns and Mistique charged in after him, eyes darting round the vast chamber as they searched for their first target. Morgan was reclining on embroidered cushions with a beautiful young woman, drinking wine from a silver goblet, and whispering something into her ear as she giggled helplessly. Half a dozen men-at-arms were playing cards at a table in a far corner. There was no sign of any sorcerer.

The men at the table looked round, startled, as the doors burst open, and then scrambled to their feet, grabbing for their swords. Morgan pushed aside his scantily clad companion and struggled to get to his feet, slipping and sliding on the cushions. Hawk sprinted forward, hoping to get to Morgan before the men-at-arms could reach him, but Morgan finally got his feet under him and ran for the far door. Thin streamers of mist shot past Hawk and wrapped themselves around Morgan, bringing him crashing to the floor. The far door flew open, revealing a tall, gaunt-faced man dressed in sorcerer's black. He gestured quickly, and the misty coils holding Morgan disappeared.

Hawk and Burns threw themselves at the charging men-at-arms. Hawk cut down the first two to reach him with savage sweeps of his axe. Blood pooled thickly on the floor as he stepped quickly over the writhing bodies to attack the next man. They stood face to face for a moment, exchanging cut and thrust and parry, but the man-at-arms was no match for Hawk's cold fury, and both of them knew it. The swordsman began to back away, and Hawk went after him. He swung his axe with vicious skill, and then caught a glimpse of flashing steel out of the corner of his eye. He threw himself to one side, and the young woman's sword just missed him. Hawk kicked the man-at-arms in the knee, elbowed him in the face, and turned quickly to face the young woman as she attacked him with just as much skill as the man-at-arms. Hawk wondered briefly where she'd hidden a sword in such a brief outfit, and then was forced to give her his full attention as she pressed home her attack.

She was good with a sword, and worse still, fresh and rested, while he was fighting off a long day's fatigue. He stood his ground, swinging his axe with both hands, but she deflected most of his blows and easily dodged the rest. Once again Hawk caught a glimpse of movement at his side, and sidestepped quickly as the man-at-arms he'd elbowed threw himself forward and accidentally impaled himself on the young woman's sword. She froze in shock, and Hawk slammed the butt of his axe against her head. She fell to the floor without a murmur and lay still. Hawk glowered down at her. If he'd had any sense, he'd have killed her while he had the chance, but he always was too chivalrous for his own good. Besides, he rationalized, she might answer questions that Morgan wouldn't.

He looked around him, suddenly aware the room was strangely quiet. Burns had dealt with the other men-at-arms, and was standing over his last kill, breathing heavily and checking himself for wounds. There didn't seem to be anything serious. Hawk grinned. There was a lot to be said for the advantage of surprise, not to mention the adrenalin provided by extreme desperation.

He looked across at Mistique, who was standing very still, her face cold, her eyes locked on the other sorcerer, still standing by the far door. Stray magic spat and sparkled on the air between them.

Mists curled and twisted around Mistique like unfinished ghosts, and then leapt forward with heart-stopping speed, only to dissipate and fall apart before they could reach the sorcerer. He raised his hand in a short, casual gesture and all around Mistique the floor bulged suddenly upwards, tearing itself apart. The jagged wood erupted up into thick twisting branches that clutched at the air like gnarled fingers. Barbed thorns thrust out of the crackling wood as the branches stretched towards Mistique. Thick tendrils of mist boiled off the sorceress, and shot forward to engulf the lengthening branches. The unliving wood cracked and splintered as the mists writhed, ripping the branches apart. Beads of sweat appeared on the sorcerer's face as the mists advanced on him. Sharp wooden stalagmites thrust out of the floor and wall around Mistique, piercing the air with razored points, but none of them came close to touching her. A pearly haze built around the sorcerer, thickening inexorably into a fog that swallowed him up. There was a single, choked cry from inside the fog, and then silence. The fog quickly cleared, dispersed by a sourceless wind, and there was no trace of the sorcerer anywhere. Hawk decided not to ask; he didn't think he wanted to know. Mistique glanced across at him.

"That's what comes of overspecialisation. If he hadn't limited himself to working with wood, he might have been able to do some real damage."

"You only work with mists," Hawk pointed out, striding quickly over to Morgan, who was still lying where he'd fallen.

"Mists are different," said Mistique. "You can do a lot with mists."

Hawk shrugged, grabbed Morgan by the collar, and dragged him to his feet. The drug baron twisted suddenly, a knife gleaming in his hand. Hawk let go and jumped back, sucking in his gut, and the knife ripped through his furs and out again without touching him. Morgan drew back his hand for another thrust, and Hawk caught him with a straight-finger jab just below the breastbone. Morgan's face paled, and the knife slipped from his numb fingers. Hawk grabbed him by the shirt-front and slammed him back against the nearest wall. He put his face close to Morgan's and showed the drug baron his death's-head smile.

"Talk to me, Morgan."

"What . . . what do you want to know?" Morgan fought to keep his voice even, but he couldn't face Hawk's cold gaze. He looked over Hawk's shoulder at Burns and Mistique, standing together, and his face paled even more.

"Let's start with the drug," said Hawk. "The super-chacal. Where is it?"

"In one of the back rooms here." Morgan looked reluctantly back at Hawk. "There are lots of empty rooms here. More than I can ever use."

"Have you started moving it yet?"

"No, we've been having difficulties setting up a new distribution network, thanks to your interference."

"It's nice to be appreciated," said Hawk. "Now let's talk about the drug itself. This super-chacal is something new. You didn't come up with it yourself. Developing a new drug takes lots of time and money, not to mention a staff of high-level alchemists in their own private lab. And that's out of your league, Morgan. So how did you get your hands on it?"

Morgan tried to shrug, but Hawk had too tight a hold on him. "It came in through the Docks, disguised as spices. All I had to do was make sure it hadn't been cut with anything, then package it and make the connection with the distributors. The drug itself was financed by outside money."

Hawk frowned thoughtfully. "Outside money . . . Outside Haven, or outside the Low Kingdoms?"

"Didn't know. Didn't care. Money's money; I don't give a damn where it comes from. This sounded like a good deal, so I went for it. I never got to talk to the real backers; they always worked through middlemen. I can give you their names if you want, but it won't do you any good. They'll have left Haven by now. I'd planned to be long gone myself, once the drug hit the streets."

"You really are a piece of slime, you know that?" Hawk thrust his face up close before Morgan's, and the drug baron tried to shrink back into the solid wall. Hawk's voice was calm and even, but his face held a bitter rage only barely held in check. "You knew what the drug was, and what it would do to anyone who took it. You knew that once the super-chacal hit the streets, there'd be a bloodbath that would tear Haven apart. But you went ahead with it anyway."

Morgan squirmed uncomfortably. "Come on, Hawk, if I hadn't gone for it, someone else would have. You're exaggerating the dangers. So we lose a few scum from the streets. So what? No one who really matters would have been hurt. And there's millions to be made from this drug. Once word gets out, everyone will want to try it. It gives a kind of hit no one's ever been able to deliver before. Even the weakest man can become strong enough and brave enough to get back at everyone who's ever done him down. Millions of ducats, Hawk. Think of it. It's not too late; you can still cut yourself in. There's enough money in this for everyone."

Hawk grinned at Morgan, and he shut up. "No deals, Morgan. Now then, you've done very well, so far. Just one more question, and I'll be finished with you. Answer it correctly, and you'll live to stand trial. You bought off a lot of people in the Guard while setting up this deal, but I'm interested in one name in particular. You bought yourself a Guard Captain. You know who I mean; the well-respected Captain, the one who no one would suspect. The one who made your drugs vanish from Guard Headquarters. I want to know who that Captain is. I want to know very badly. So you tell me the name, Morgan, or I swear I'll cut you into pieces right here and now."

"Hawk, you can't do this," said Burns. "It's inhuman."

"Shut up, Burns."

"He has to stand trial, Hawk. He'll tell us everything we need to know, under a truthspell."

"I need to know now! Talk to me, Morgan!"

"Stop it, Hawk! I won't stand for this!"

Hawk half turned to shout at Burns, and Morgan brought his knee up sharply into Hawk's groin. Air whistled in his throat as he fell backwards, momentarily paralysed by the pain. Morgan made a dash for the far door, but Mistique put herself between him and the door. Mists boiled up off her outstretched hands. Morgan produced another knife from somewhere and lunged at her. Burns ran him through from behind with his sword. Morgan sank slowly to his knees, still holding onto his knife. He coughed painfully, and blood ran thickly from his mouth. He fell forward and lay still, and Burns pulled his sword free. He knelt down beside the body, tried for a pulse at the neck, and shook his head. He got to his feet again, and a hand grabbed his shoulder from behind. He looked round, startled, and Hawk punched him in the mouth. Burns stumbled backwards, blood spilling down his chin. Hawk went after him, but Mistique grabbed him from behind and held him firmly.

"Stop it, Hawk! That's enough!"

Hawk struggled fiercely, but he was still weakened by Morgan's attack and he couldn't break her grip. His gaze was fixed on Burns. "You stupid bastard! I told you we needed him alive! How is he going to answer questions now?"

"I'm sorry," said Burns indistinctly, wiping blood from his mouth with the back of his hand. "I didn't think . . . I just saw him lunging at Mistique, and I really thought he was going to kill her. . . ."

"I could have handled him," said Mistique.

"Yes, I'm sure you could have," said Burns, looking at the blood smeared across his hand. "I didn't think . . . I'm sorry."

"Damn you," said Hawk. "What are we going to do now? He was the only one who knew all the names." He shook his head sickly, then took a deep breath and let it out slowly. "It's all right, Mistique, you can let me go now. I'm all right."

She let him go, and stood back. Hawk moved over to Morgan's body and knelt down beside it, wincing as pain shot through him. He'd managed to take some of Morgan's kneeing on his thigh, but the pain was still bad enough to make him move like an old man. He tried for a pulse, but couldn't find one. He searched the body slowly and methodically, but didn't come up with anything useful, apart from a small bunch of keys. He got to his feet again, with a little help from Mistique.

"At least we've got the drugs back," he said brusquely. "And this time I'll make sure they don't go missing, even if I have to feed every damn package to the incinerator myself."

"We ought to search the place before we go," said Burns. "There's always the chance he kept records of who was working for him, and who he was paying off."

Hawk nodded curtly. "He probably had more sense than to leave something like that just lying about, but it's worth a look. Don't move anything, though. We'll leave the real search to the experts. Place is probably rigged with booby traps." A sudden thought struck him and he looked quickly at Mistique. "Or is this place going to collapse around our ears like the other one?"

The sorceress shook her head. "Solid as rock. Whoever set up this place knew what he was doing."

They headed for the far door, Mistique staying close by Hawk in case he needed to lean on her again. Burns kept a tactful distance. The sorceress cleared her throat uncertainly.

"Hawk . . . would you really have used your axe on Morgan?"

He smiled slightly. "I was bluffing. Mostly. I'm not really as bad as my reputation makes out."

"You convinced me," said Mistique. "I've never seen anyone look so mad."

"I wanted the name."

"Hawk," said Mistique gently. "We already know the name."

"So, did you find anything?" asked Commander Glen, leaning forward over his desk and staring intently at Hawk and Burns.

Hawk shook his head. "Nothing useful. And Morgan didn't strike me as dumb enough to commit anything incriminating to paper anyway."

Glen sniffed, and leaned back in his chair. "You're probably right. At least you had enough restraint not to wreck the place, for a change—even if you didn't leave anyone alive to answer questions."

"What about the man-at-arms Mistique put to sleep?" said Burns. "And the woman Hawk knocked out?"

"Hired muscle," said Glen dismissively. "They weren't far enough in to know anything useful. And speaking of Mistique, where is she? I want to hear her report, too."

Hawk and Burns stared over Glen's head at the wall behind him. "She said she'd look in later," said Hawk. "She's . . . rather busy at the moment." He lowered his gaze abruptly, and fixed Glen with his single, cold eye. "Commander, there's something I need to discuss with you."

"Yes," said Glen. "We have to talk about Captain Fisher. I've been hearing stories about her for some time now. As long as they were just stories I could afford to ignore them. You and Fisher were a good team; you got results. But I can't ignore this, Hawk. She's betrayed the security of the Peace Talks, and gone on the run. We have no idea where she is, or what she might be planning. And now there's mounting evidence that she's been working for Morgan all along."

"I don't believe that," said Hawk. "I don't believe any of it."

Glen looked at him steadily. "She's gone rogue, Hawk. I have issued a warrant for her arrest. There's a reward of five thousand ducats for anyone who brings her in, dead or alive."

For a moment Hawk just looked back at him, his scarred face cold and impassive, saying nothing. "I'll find her," he said finally. "I'll find her, and bring her in. Call off your dogs, Commander."

"I can't do that, Hawk. It's out of my hands now. And I can't let you go, either. You did a good job in recovering the super-chacal, but you upset a great many prominent people in the process. If you'd brought Morgan in alive, no one would have said anything, but as it is . . ."

"That was my fault, Commander," said Burns, but Hawk and Glen didn't even look at him.

"Now that Fisher's gone rogue," said Glen, "you've become suspect too, Hawk, through your relationship with her. Too many things have gone wrong around you just lately. No one trusts you anymore. I have a warrant for your arrest too, Hawk. I'm sorry."

"You've got to let me find Fisher," said Hawk. "Please. Let me bring her in, and we'll prove our innocence."

"I'm sorry," said Glen. "I have my orders. Give me your axe, please."

Hawk drew his axe, and the room suddenly became very tense. He hefted the weapon in his hand a moment, and then put it down on Glen's desk. The Commander relaxed a little, and Hawk hit him with a vicious left uppercut. Glen flew backwards out of his chair, slammed into the wall behind his desk, and slid unconscious to the floor. Burns opened his mouth to yell something, his hand already reaching for his sword. Hawk spun round, grabbed up his axe, and hit Burns across the head with the flat of the blade while Burns was still drawing his sword. He fell to the floor and lay there motionless, groaning quietly.

Hawk would have liked to tie them both up, but a quick glance around showed him nothing he could use as a rope, and he didn't have the time, anyway. He hauled them both into Glen's private washroom, and locked the door on them. He took a last quick look round, and then left Glen's office and made his way casually through Headquarters to the main entrance. He smiled and nodded to people he passed, and they smiled and muttered automatically in return. Hawk kept his face calm, but his thoughts were in a turmoil. He had to find Isobel before anyone else did. He couldn't trust anyone else with the job.

Isobel . . . I'm coming for you.

9

Under the Masks

Fisher moved quietly through the back streets, trudging doggedly through the snow and slush, with her head bowed. The tattered grey cloak didn't do much to keep out the cold, but with the hood pulled well forward there was no way anyone was going to recognise her. After all, who would expect the bold and dashing Captain Fisher to be skulking through the worst part of town in rags she wouldn't normally have used to polish her boots? She seethed inwardly at the indignity, but kept her outer demeanour carefully calm and unobtrusive. Her disguise would only hold up as long as no one challenged it, and there were a hell of a lot of people who'd be only too happy to turn her in for whatever reward was currently on her head.

Fisher had no doubt there was a reward. The Powers That Be needed a scapegoat, and she was tailor-made for the role. She could plead her innocence till she was blue in the face, but no one would give a damn. She had to be found guilty so that the Outremer delegates would be reassured and the Peace Talks could go on. They'd told her right from the beginning that she was expendable. Fisher grinned fiercely. That was their opinion. If they wanted her to be a rogue, she'd be one. And anyone who got in her way was going to regret it.

She slowed her pace slightly as two ragged figures

appeared out of a dark alley mouth and moved casually towards her. She caught brief glimpses of the knives half hidden under their cloaks, and turned to face them. She'd obviously overdone the unthreatening aspect of her disguise and made herself look an easy target. Fisher scowled. She couldn't afford to fight them; at best it would draw attention to her, particularly when she won, and at worst it might actually give away who she was. But she couldn't hope for any help, either. Not in the Northside. She swore under her breath, and let her hand move to her sword under cover of the cloak. There was never a bloody Constable around when you needed one.

The two bravos moved to block her path, and she came to a halt. She pushed back her cloak to reveal the sword at her side, and lifted her head to give them her best glare. She'd put a lot of work and practice into that glare, and it had always served her well in the past. It suggested she was one hundred per cent crazy, barely under control, and violent with it. The two bravos took in the glare and the sword, looked at each other, and then made their knives disappear, and moved casually off in another direction, as though they'd intended to go that way all along. Fisher let her cloak fall back to cover the sword, pulled her hood even lower over her face, and continued on her way, trying not to look too much in a hurry.

She had to think of somewhere to go, somewhere she could hole up for a while till she could figure some way to get out of the city. She couldn't go home; it was the first place they'd think of, and was probably crawling with Guards by now, ransacking every room in search of evidence that wasn't there. A slow, sullen anger burned in her, at the thought of strangers trampling through her house, but she knew there was no point in brooding over it. Or the treasured possessions she'd have to leave behind when she finally found a way out of the city.

She had to find somewhere she could stop and think, somewhere safe. And there were all sorts of things she'd have to get her hands on, things she'd need just to survive out in the wilds of the Low Kingdoms, in the dead of winter.

Starting with a decent fur cloak. The cold cut right through the thin grey one she had now. And she'd need a horse and provisions . . . and a dozen other things, none of which she had the money to buy. Her money was back at the house. What there was of it.

Her pace slowed as her thoughts churned furiously. She wasn't used to having to plan ahead. That had always been Hawk's responsibility. Hawk. The name cut at her briefly, like a razor drawn against unsuspecting skin. She wanted to go to him so badly, but she didn't dare. Everything she'd heard since she hit the streets suggested that Hawk had gone berserk, fighting and killing anyone who got between him and Morgan. Something bad must have happened, something so awful he no longer cared what happened to him as long as he got to Morgan. Her first impulse had been to find him and fight at his side, but she couldn't do that. By now there had to be a small army of Guards on her tail, and she'd be leading them straight to Hawk. And if he really had gone berserk, he'd die rather than be stopped.

She couldn't let that happen.

There must be somewhere she could go, somewhere they wouldn't think of looking. She trudged on, head down, not looking where she was going, as her mind floundered from one possibility to another before finally, reluctantly, settling on one. The Tolling Bell was a rancid little tavern, tucked away at the back of nowhere. The kind of place where they sold illegally strong drinks and the bartender had little conversation and even less of a memory for faces. Fisher had used the place before, when she needed to get away by herself for a while. When she'd had a row with Hawk, or just needed to be alone with her thoughts. She'd always taken pains to disguise her identity, so no one could find her till she was ready to be found. The Tolling Bell . . . Yes . . . she could be there in half an hour.

Her head snapped up, suddenly alert as she heard tramping feet heading towards her. Six Guard Constables were moving purposefully in her direction. She quickly dropped her head again, and hunched over under her cloak to make herself look smaller. Her hand moved unobtrusively to the sword at her side. Six-to-one odds, and no one to watch her back. Bad odds, but she'd faced worse in her time. She glanced cautiously around for possible escape routes, and only then realised the Guards weren't actually looking at her. Hope flared in her again, and she shrank back against the wall as the Guards tramped past, doing her best to look insignificant and harmless. The Constables hardly glanced at her as they passed, and continued on their way. Fisher waited where she was, listening to the sound of the footsteps dying gradually away, and then moved slowly on, careful not to look behind her. Her back crawled in anticipation of a sudden sword thrust, but it never came. She finally allowed herself to glance back over her shoulder, and found the Constables were almost out of sight at the end of the street. Her breath began to come a little more easily, and she increased her pace. She'd be safe at The Tolling Bell. For a while. She could sit down, and rest, and think. And just maybe she'd be able to see a way out of this mess.

Hawk strode angrily down the main street, pulling his ratty brown cloak tightly about him. The cold cut through the ragged cloth as though it weren't there, but at least the hood concealed his face, as long as he remembered to keep his head bowed. Someone had to have found Glen and Burns by now, which meant word would soon be circulating on the streets that Hawk was fair game for anyone who felt like going after him. And with the kind of reward the Guard would be offering, there'd be no shortage of volunteers. Most of the usual bounty hunters would have more sense than to go after Captain Hawk, but there were always some stupid enough to take any risk, for a chance at the big money. And if enough of them got together, they might just manage it.

Hawk scowled, and peered unobtrusively about him. They were after Fisher too. He had to find her, before anyone else did. Find her, and find out what had happened. Why she'd betrayed Haven, and the Guard. And him. There had to be a reason, a good reason. He believed that implicitly, because to think anything else would drive him insane. He trusted

Isobel, but all the evidence pointed to her guilt. As a Guard, he'd learned to rely on the evidence before anything else, and never to trust his instincts or his feelings until he had hard evidence to back them up. But this was different. This was Isobel. He had to find her and hear her explanation. And then he'd know what to do next.

Though really, deep down, he'd already decided what he was going to do. Whatever she said, whatever she'd done; it didn't matter. Once before he'd given up everything he had for her sake, and he wouldn't hesitate to do it again if he had to. There were other cities, other countries they could go to, and it wouldn't be the first time they'd had to change their names.

But he had to find her soon, before the Guard did. She wouldn't go to any of her usual haunts; too many other people knew about them. There had to be some place she'd regard as safe, some place she'd think no one knew about but her. . . . The Tolling Bell. That had to be it. Isobel often disappeared there when she lost an argument or was feeling broody.

A shout went up not too far away, as a sudden gust of wind caught the edge of his hood and flipped it back, revealing his face. Hawk pulled the hood back into position, but the damage had been done. Two Guard Constables were running towards him, swords drawn. Hawk looked quickly around for an escape route, but they were all blocked by curious onlookers eager for some free entertainment. Hawk cursed unemotionally, straightened up, and drew his axe. He shrugged his cloak back out of the way and stamped the snow flat to give him better footing. He hefted his axe thoughtfully, and waited for the two Constables to come within range. He didn't want to kill them if he could avoid it. They were just doing their job. As far as they were concerned, he was a rogue and a traitor. But he couldn't let them stop him. Isobel's life might depend on his getting to her before anyone else did.

The Constables slowed their pace as they drew near Hawk, and moved apart to take him from two directions at once. Hawk picked the nearest one, and launched himself forward. He ducked under the Constable's wild swing, the sword blade tugging briefly at the top of his hood, and slammed his shoulder into the Constable's gut. The man folded in half and fell away, gasping for air. Hawk clubbed him forcefully across the back of the head with the butt of his axe, and then spun round just in time to block an attack from the other Constable.

The two of them stamped back and forth, feinting and withdrawing, each trying to make the other commit himself. Hawk faked a stumble, and went down on one knee. The Constable immediately fell back a step, too old a hand to be taken in by such an obvious stunt, and Hawk hit him in the face with the handful of snow he'd palmed when he went down. The Constable staggered back, lashing out blindly with his sword while he tried to claw the snow out of his eyes with his free hand. Hawk timed it carefully, stepped in during a brief moment when the Constable left himself open, and kicked him in the groin.

The Constable went down without a sound, and Hawk clubbed him unconscious. He nodded once, satisfied, and then froze as a shout went up again, some way behind him. He looked round and saw six more Constables charging down the street towards him. Hawk turned on his heel and ran for the nearest alleyway. If he had to take on six-to-one odds with no one to guard his back, someone was definitely going to end up dead. Quite possibly him. The people in the alley mouth scattered as he bore down on them axe in hand, and he plunged past them into the concealing gloom of the narrow passageway. His best bet was to try and lose his pursuers in the maze of back streets and cul de sacs. He knew this area, and the odds were they didn't. He just hoped he wouldn't have to outrun them. He was already short of breath. It had been a long day, and the end was nowhere in sight.

He scowled to himself as he ran. Running from a mere six-to-one odds. If this got out, he'd never live it down.

Captain ap Owen watched with interest as Commander Glen sat glowering behind his desk, painfully growling orders to a steady stream of visitors. He kept an ice pack pressed against his face. A quite spectacular bruise was spreading across his jaw and peeking round the edges of the ice pack. People came and went in sudden rushes and flurries, darting into the office to deliver updated reports and possible sightings, and then quickly disappearing before Glen could turn his glare on them. But for all their bustle and effort, it was clear they were no nearer locating Hawk or Fisher.

"They can't just have vanished," protested Captain Burns, pacing back and forth, and occasionally raising a hand to feel gingerly at the back of his head. He claimed to have a hell of a bump there, but no one else had seen it. Ap Owen thought it was probably more hurt pride than anything else. Burns glared at ap Owen as though it were all his fault, and ap Owen quickly looked away, somehow keeping a smile off his face. It had to be said, he'd never much cared for Burns. Too interested in looking good, that one. Probably had a great career ahead of him—in administration.

"We'll find them," said Glen slowly, trying hard not to move his mouth when he spoke. "We've got their house staked out, and all their usual haunts. The city Gates have been sealed, so they can't get out of Haven. All we have to do now is run them to ground . . ." He broke off abruptly as a wave of pain hit him, but his eyes were still hot and furious.

"We're leaning on all the usual informants," said ap Owen. "Most of them are falling over themselves at a chance to do Hawk and Fisher some dirt. Those two have made an awful lot of enemies during their short time in Haven."

Burns sniffed. "No honour among thieves. Or traitors."

Ap Owen raised an eyebrow. "That's hardly fair, Burns. Up until now, Hawk and Fisher have always had an exemplary reputation."

"You have got to be joking. Everyone knows about the brutal tactics they use. They don't care who they hurt or intimidate, and they kill anyone who gets in their way. I've even heard it said they plant evidence and manufacture confessions, just to make their arrest rate look good. They're no better than thugs in uniform."

"They always upheld the law."

"When it suited them," said Burns. "Anybody can be bought, for the right price."

Ap Owen shrugged unhappily, and looked across at Glen. "With respect, Commander, I think our quarry have more than enough sense to keep clear of all their usual haunts. Is there anywhere they might go, that they might think we don't know about? You were with Hawk all day, Burns. Did he mention any place to you?"

"If he had, I'd have said so!" snapped Burns. "Why aren't you out there looking for them? You've got twenty men under you. Why aren't you out combing the streets?"

"What's the point?" said ap Owen mildly. "We've got half an army out there as it is; adding my people to that pack would only give them someone else to trip over. Besides, I don't want my men wandering aimlessly about in the cold, or they won't be worth spit when we finally get a chance to arrest Hawk or Fisher. Or both. In fact, the more I think about it, the more sure I am they'll have joined up by now. They always were very devoted to each other."

"I don't know," said Glen indistinctly, from behind his ice pack. "Hawk seemed honestly shocked when he heard the news about Fisher's treachery. I think there's a real chance he may not be involved in the treason himself."

"If he wasn't a traitor before, he is now," said Burns. "He's defied lawful orders and assaulted a superior officer. And right now you can bet he's doing his utmost to help the traitor Fisher to escape justice. Even though her actions may have helped to start a war."

"Calm down," said ap Owen. "It isn't that bad. Yet. The delegates are still talking to each other, even if it's not on an official basis at the moment. There's still hope. In the meantime, guilty or not, I think we can assume Hawk is doing his best to locate Fisher. And since he's much more likely to figure out where she's hidden herself than we are, I think we can also assume that when we finally catch up with them, they're going to be together. And together, they're the most formidable fighting machine Haven has ever seen. I'm not sure I can take them, even with twenty men under me. Which is why, Captain Burns, my men are staying here, warm and rested, until they're needed. I don't want them worn out from chasing round Haven after every unconfirmed sighting."

"Thank you, Captain," said Glen heavily. "I think you've made your point." He scowled at ap Owen and Burns, and then stared unseeingly at the papers on his desk, his fingers drumming quietly as he thought. "Hawk said something once, about Fisher having a special place to go to be on her own, when she wanted to get away from everything. He told me about it one time, when we were looking for her in an emergency and couldn't find her. It was an inn. The something Bell. The Tolling Bell, that was it."

"What district?" said ap Owen.

"How the hell should I know? Find out!"

Ap Owen rose to his feet. "It's got to be somewhere near their home. Shouldn't be too hard to find someone here who lives in that area. I'll let you know the minute I've got word, Commander; then I'll move in with my men while you have the area surrounded. Maybe we can talk Hawk and Fisher into giving up. I don't see any point in getting my people killed if I can avoid it."

"It's not as simple as that," said Glen slowly. "I have my orders, Captain ap Owen, and I'm passing them on to you. Hawk and Fisher are to be brought in dead. We're not interested in their capture or surrender. Our superiors have decided that they can't be allowed to stand trial. They know too many secrets, too many things the Council can't afford to have discussed in public. So Hawk and Fisher are going to die resisting arrest. That's the way our superiors want it, and that's the way it's going to be. Understand?"

"Yes, Commander," said ap Owen. "I understand. Now, if you'll excuse me . . ."

"I'm going with you," said Burns. "I have a personal stake in this."

Ap Owen glanced at Commander Glen, who nodded brusquely. Ap Owen crossed over to the door without looking at Burns, and left the Commander's office. Burns followed him out. Glen stared at the papers on his desk for a long time before returning to his work.

Fisher slipped into The Tolling Bell tavern with her hood pulled low, and ordered an ale by pointing and grunting. The bartender drew her off a pint without commenting. You got all sorts in The Tolling Bell. Fisher paid for her drink and quickly settled herself in a dark corner, careful to avoid her usual booth. She took a long swallow of the bitter ale, wiped the froth from her upper lip with care, so as not to disturb her hood, and only then allowed herself to relax a little. She'd always thought of The Bell as a sanctuary, a place apart from the cares and duties of her life, and now she needed that feeling more than ever. She looked around casually, checking the place out.

The inn was quiet, not surprising given the time of day, with only a dozen or so customers. Fisher recognised all of them as regulars. They'd mind their own business. They always did.

Hawk's gone berserk. He's killing anyone who gets in his way.

Fisher squeezed her eyes shut. She didn't want to believe that what she'd heard was true, but it could be. It could be. And if it were . . . she didn't know what to do for the best. She couldn't let him go on as he was. If he really had gone berserk, innocent people might get hurt, even killed. She couldn't risk looking for him herself; she might unknowingly lead the Guard right to him. But she couldn't just abandon him, either. She had to do something . . . something, while there was still time.

In the street outside, Hawk leaned against a wall and looked casually about him. No one seemed to be paying him any untoward attention. He was pretty sure he hadn't been followed since he shook off the pursuing Constables, but he wasn't taking any chances. He approved of Fisher's choice of inn. The Tolling Bell was quiet, off the beaten track and nicely anonymous. Not at all the kind of place you'd expect to find Captains Hawk and Fisher. He took one last look around, pulled his hood even lower, and ducked in through the open doorway.

He strolled over to the bar, and ordered a beer by grunting and pointing. The bartender looked at him for a moment, and then drew him a pint. Hawk paid the man, put his back against the bar, and sipped his beer thoughtfully as he looked about him. The other customers ignored him completely, but one figure near the back seemed to be going out of its way to avoid looking in his direction.

Fisher's heart beat painfully fast, and she clutched her glass until her knuckles showed white. She had recognised Hawk the moment he entered the inn. She knew the way he walked, the way he moved . . . He'd spotted her. She could tell from the way his stance suddenly changed. Her thoughts raced furiously. Why was he just standing there? Had he come to take her in? Did he want Morgan so badly now, he'd even sacrifice her in return for a clear shot at the drug baron? *He's gone rogue. Killing anyone who gets in his way. Anyone.*

She shoved her chair back from the table and sprang to her feet. She swept her cloak over her shoulders, out of the way, and drew her sword. She couldn't let Hawk take her in. He didn't understand what was going on. They'd kill her, once she was safely out of the public eye, to be sure of appeasing the Outremer delegates. She couldn't let Hawk take her in.

Hawk shrugged his own cloak back out of the way, and drew his axe as she drew her sword. What little he could see of her face looked strained and desperate. *She must be a traitor. She's betrayed everyone. She betrayed you.* There were frantic scrambling sounds all around as the other customers hurried to get out of the way. A tense, echoing silence filled the room.

She's a traitor. All the evidence proves it. She drew a sword on you. You can't trust her anymore.

He's a rogue. He's gone berserk, out of control. He's killed people all over Haven. You can't trust him anymore.

Hawk slowly straightened up out of his fighting stance,

and put away his axe. He pushed back his hood, and walked slowly towards Isobel. She straightened up and lowered her sword. Hawk stopped before her, easily in reach of her sword, and smiled at her.

"It's all right, Isobel. I don't care what you've done. You must have had a good reason for it. If you don't want me with you, if you feel you have to . . . leave me behind, that's all right. I'll understand. All that matters to me is that you're safe."

Fisher slammed her sword back into its scabbard, and hugged Hawk fiercely, crushing the breath out of him. "You damned fool, Hawk! As if I could ever leave you . . ."

They clung together for a while, happy and secure in each other's arms, eyes squeezed shut, as if they could close out everything in the world except the two of them. The other customers slowly began to settle down again, though still keeping a wary eye on the embracing couple. Eventually, reluctantly, Hawk and Fisher broke apart, and stepped back to look at each other properly. Hawk's mouth twitched.

"That is a really horrible-looking cloak, Isobel."

"You should talk. What the hell have you been up to, Hawk? I've been hearing all kinds of crazy things about you."

Hawk grinned. "Most of them are probably true. You should hear what they've been saying about you."

They sat down together at Fisher's table, and brought each other up to date on the day's events. It took a while, not least because there were a lot of things they weren't too sure about themselves, but eventually they both ran down, and sat quietly, thinking hard. A growing murmur of conversation rose around them, as the inn's customers disappointedly decided that there wasn't going to be any more action after all.

"Somebody's been setting us up," said Hawk finally. "Both of us. We've been led around by the nose all day long, and we were so tied up in our own concerns we never even noticed. But the way things are, no one's going to believe us, no matter what we say. You know, we could still make a run for it. I know a forger who could knock us out new identities in under an hour."

Fisher looked at him. "Do you want to run?"

"Well, no, not really, but I thought you . . ."

"That was different. I thought I was on my own then. But now . . ."

"Right," said Hawk. "No one sets us up and gets away with it. The trouble is, who the hell did it to us? I thought for a long time it was Morgan, but that turned out not to be the case."

"Pity," said Fisher. "It would have simplified things. He said the drug was developed by *outside* money . . . so presumably the people behind Morgan are our real enemies. Whoever they are. It's not just the drug; they've got to be connected with the Peace Talks in some way as well. Maybe they were banking on the chaos the super-chacal would cause to break up the Talks, or at least keep the Guard so occupied they couldn't protect the delegates properly. Wait a minute . . . wait just a minute. All that talk of *outside* money could refer to outside the Low Kingdoms; meaning Outremer."

"Right," said Hawk. "I thought that as well. We need a wedge, something or someone we can use to force open this case and let in a little light. Look, just because you're not a traitor, it doesn't mean there isn't one. Someone removed those drugs from Headquarters, and sabotaged the Talks by revealing the house's location and the co-ordinates of the pocket dimension. Who is there that's been as closely involved in this case as you and I, and had the opportunity to do all the things you've been accused of doing?"

"If the rumours are to be believed, it's a Guard Captain," said Fisher, scowling thoughtfully into her drink. "A well-respected Captain, too honest and too trusted ever to be suspected. But the only other Captain in this case is . . ." A sudden inspiration stirred in her, and she stared at Hawk, her eyes widening. "No, it couldn't be. Not him. Not *Burns*."

"Why not? He had the opportunity." Hawk nodded grimly, his thoughts racing furiously. "It has to be him; he fits all the facts. And remember, one of Morgan's people at the drug factory said he recognised one of the Captains who took part in the raid as someone who worked for Morgan. He actually fingered you, but presumably by then he'd been got at. So, if it wasn't you, it had to be one of the other Captains. We can forget Doughty because he's dead, and we know it wasn't us, so that just leaves Burns! Dammit, I always thought he was too good to be true!"

"Wait a minute," said Fisher. "Let's not get carried away with this. How could Burns have sabotaged the Peace Talks?"

Hawk frowned. "It wouldn't have been difficult for him to get the information. He's been in and out of Headquarters all day, just like us. I feel like an idiot, Isobel. It's no wonder I've been walking into traps all day; Burns must have been reporting our position every time my back was turned!"

"It also explains why he killed Morgan," said Fisher. "He was afraid Morgan might finger him, as a way of saving his own neck. We've found our traitor, Hawk. Burns is behind everything bad that's happened to us today."

"Never liked him," said Hawk. "I wish now I'd hit him harder, when I had the chance."

"A well-respected Captain that no one would suspect. The rumours were right about that, at any rate. I never even heard a whisper about corruption concerning Burns." Fisher frowned suddenly. "You know, Hawk, this isn't going to be easy to prove. Who's going to take the word of two suspected traitors and renegades like us against a paragon of virtue like Burns?"

"We'll just have to find him, and persuade him to tell them the truth."

"No rough stuff, Hawk. He'd only claim he was intimidated into saying what we wanted him to say, and with our reputation, they'd believe him. We need evidence. Hard evidence."

"All right, but first we've got to find him. And that's not going to be easy either. He could be anywhere in Haven. Where are we supposed to start looking?"

"Right here," said Burns.

They looked up quickly, hands dropping to their weapons, and there was Burns standing by the bar, with ap Owen beside him. Guard Constables were filing quickly into the inn, swords at the ready. Once again the customers scrambled to get out of the way. Hawk and Fisher rose slowly to their feet and moved away from the table, ostentatiously keeping their hands well away from their weapons. More Guards entered the inn. Hawk counted twenty in all. If the situation hadn't been so grim, Hawk might have felt flattered they'd felt it necessary to send so many men after him and Isobel. As it was, he was more interested in trying to spot a quick escape route.

"Getting old, Hawk," said Burns casually. "You weren't even bothering to watch the door. There was a time we wouldn't have caught you this easily."

"We're not caught yet," said Hawk. "But I'm glad you're here, Burns. There's a lot of things Isobel and I want to discuss with you."

"The time for talk is over," said Burns. "In fact, your time has just run out."

"Drop your weapons on the floor, please," said ap Owen steadily. "You're under arrest, Captains."

Burns looked around, startled, and glared at ap Owen. "Those were not our orders! You obey Commander Glen's orders, or I'll have you put under arrest!" He gestured quickly to the watching Constables. "You have your instructions. Kill them both."

Hawk's axe was suddenly in his hands, the heavy blade gleaming hungrily in the lamplight. Fisher stood at his side, sword at the ready. Hawk grinned nastily at the other Guards.

"When you're ready, gentlemen. Who wants to die first?"

The Guards looked at each other. Nobody moved.

"I think we'll be leaving now," said Hawk calmly. "If anyone tries to follow us, I'll take it as a personal insult. Now, stand clear of the door."

He almost brought it off. He was Hawk, after all. But Burns suddenly stepped forward, sword in hand, and his angry voice broke the atmosphere.

"What the hell are you waiting for?" he said to his men. "You outnumber them ten to one, and they're both dog-tired from chasing round the city all day! Now carry out your orders, or I swear I'll see every man of you arrested for aiding and abetting known traitors!"

The Constables' faces hardened, and they moved slowly forward, fanning out to attack Hawk and Fisher from as many sides as possible. Hawk and Fisher moved quickly to stand back to back. Fisher looked appealingly at Captain ap Owen.

"Listen to me, ap Owen. You know this isn't right. This whole thing's a setup. There are things going on here you don't know about. Listen to me, please, for Haven's sake."

Ap Owen looked at her uncertainly. Burns glared at ap Owen.

"Don't listen to her. The bitch would say anything to save her neck."

"Watch your mouth, Burns," said ap Owen. "Stay where you are, men. No one is to start anything without my order. Unless any of you really want to go one-on-one with Captain Hawk."

The Constables lowered their swords and relaxed a little, some of them looking openly relieved. Burns started to say something angrily, and then stopped when he realised ap Owen's sword was pressed against his side.

"I think we've heard enough from you, Captain Burns," said ap Owen. "Now please be quiet, while I listen to what Captain Fisher has to say."

"To start with," said Fisher, "take a look at Hawk. Does he really look like he's gone kill-crazy? The only person here who fits that description is Burns, the very person who's been supplying all the evidence against Hawk. As for me, I was set up. Do you really think I'd have stuck around to defend the Talks if I'd known there was an army of mercenaries on the way? Or retreated into the pocket dimension with you if I'd known it was going to be under attack, too? No, there's only one traitor here, and he's standing right beside you."

"You see," said Burns. "I told you she'd say anything. She'll be accusing you next. We have to kill them, or the Outremer delegates will walk out! Dammit, ap Owen, you follow your orders or I swear I'll see you hanged as a traitor yourself!"

"Oh, shut up," said ap Owen. "I'm getting really tired of the sound of your voice, Burns." He looked at Hawk and Fisher. "Let's assume, just for the moment, that there may be something in what you say. That buys you a reprieve. But I've still got to take you in. If you'll hand over your weapons, I give you my word that I'll get you back to Headquarters alive and unharmed, and you can tell your story to Commander Glen. Sound fair to you?"

"Very fair," said Fisher. "I promise you, you won't regret this."

Ap Owen smiled slightly. "I'm already regretting it. Ah hell; I was never that interested in promotion anyway."

Burns stepped forward suddenly and addressed the Constables, who were stirring uneasily and looking at each other. "Men, Commander Glen himself put me in charge of you, along with ap Owen. You know what your orders are. Now, whose orders are you going to follow—your Commander's, or a Captain who is clearly allied with the traitors Hawk and Fisher?"

The Guards looked at ap Owen, and then back at Burns. They didn't have to say anything; Burns could see the decision in their faces. They didn't trust him, and they weren't going to take on Hawk and Fisher if they didn't have to. Burns turned suddenly, slapped ap Owen's sword aside, and ran for the door. The Constables moved instinctively to stop him, and Burns cut about him viciously with his sword. Hawk and Fisher charged after him. Men fell screaming as blood flew on the air. Burns plunged forward, his eyes fixed on the door.

He'd almost made it when Hawk brought him down with a last, desperate leap. They rolled back and forth on the floor, kicking and struggling. The Constables crowded in around them, hacking and cutting at Burns, furious at his treacherous attack. Hawk fought back with his axe, as much

to protect himself as Burns. He shouted that they needed
Burns alive, but the Guards were too angry to care. Ap
Owen yelled orders that no one listened to. Fisher threw
herself into the fray, hauling Guards away from the fight
by main force and sheer determination, but there were too
many Guards between her and Hawk, and she knew it. The
Constables fought each other to get at Burns, blinded by
blood and rage. Hawk tried to get his feet under him, and
failed. Swords flew all around him, and blood pooled on the
floor. He braced himself for one last effort, and hardened
his heart at the thought of the innocent Guards he'd have
to kill. He couldn't let Burns die.

And then a thick fog boiled in through the open door,
filling the inn in a matter of moments. A hundred clammy
tentacles tore the combatants apart and held them firmly
in unyielding misty coils. There was a pause as they all
struggled futilely, and then the sorceress Mistique stepped
delicately in through the open door. Hawk relaxed and
grinned at her.

"I was wondering when you were going to turn up again."

"You didn't think I was going to miss out on the cli-
max, after all I've been through today, did you, darling?"
Mistique smiled back at him, and then looked around stern-
ly. "I'm going to let you go now. But anyone who misbe-
haves will regret it. Is that understood?"

The Constables nodded, their anger already cooling rapidly. Some of them realised they'd been fighting Hawk and
Fisher, and went pale as they considered how lucky they
were to still be alive. Mistique gestured gracefully, and the
mists fell away from everyone, dissipating quickly on the
warm air. Hawk and Fisher pushed the Guards out of the
way and knelt down beside Burns. There was a gaping
wound in his side, and a lot of blood on the floor around
him. Fisher pulled out a clean folded handkerchief and
pressed it against the wound, but it was clearly too little too
late. Burns turned his head slightly, and looked at Hawk.
His face was very pale, but his mouth and chin were red
with blood.

"Almost had you," he said quietly.

"Why, Burns?" said Hawk. "You were one of the best. Everyone said so. Why betray everything you ever believed in?"

"For the money, of course. I spent years overseeing transactions of gold and silver and precious stones, protecting men who had more money than they knew what to do with, and eventually I just decided I wanted some of that wealth for myself. I wanted some of the luxuries and comforts I saw every day and couldn't touch. Honour and honesty are all very well, but they don't pay the bills. I was going to be rich, Hawk, richer than you've ever dreamed of. Almost made it. Would have, too, if it hadn't been for you and that bitch."

"You were Morgan's contact inside the Guard, weren't you?" said Fisher impatiently.

"Of course," said Burns. "I went to Morgan and suggested it. It was perfect. Who would ever have suspected me?"

"People died because of you," said Hawk. "People who trusted you."

Burns grinned widely. There was blood on his teeth. "They shouldn't have got in my way. I killed Doughty, you know. He was there when that little bastard at the drug factory recognised me. So I killed him, and persuaded the informant to implicate Fisher instead."

"You killed your own partner?" said Fisher, shocked.

"Why not?" said Burns. "I was going to be rich. I didn't need him anymore."

"Why did you betray the Peace Talks?" said Hawk.

Burns chuckled painfully, and fresh blood spilled down his chin. "I didn't. That wasn't me. See, you're not as smart as you thought you were, are you?"

"Who was it, Burns?" said Hawk. "Who were you working for?"

"Go to hell," said Burns. He reared up, tried to spit blood at Hawk, and then the light went out of his eyes and he fell back and died.

"Great," said Hawk. "Bloody marvelous. Every time I think I've found someone who can explain what the hell's going on, they bloody up and die on me."

He closed Burns's staring eyes with a surprisingly gentle hand, and got to his feet again. He made to offer ap Owen his axe, but ap Owen shook his head. Fisher stood up, looked down at Burns a moment, and then kicked the body viciously.

"Don't," said Hawk. "He was a good man, once."

"I'm damned if I know what's happening anymore," said ap Owen. "But Burns's dying confession seemed straightforward enough, so as far as I'm concerned, you're both cleared. But you'd better stick with me until we can get back to Headquarters and make it official. There's still a lot of people out on the streets looking for you, with swords in their hands and blood in their eyes. The Council has done everything but declare open season on you both."

"We can't go back," said Hawk. "It's not over yet. You heard what Burns said; he didn't betray the Peace Talks. Someone else did that. Which means the delegates are still in danger. And the two people who should be in charge of protecting them are right here in this room with me. It's more than possible that Isobel was deliberately set up to draw attention away from the real traitor, so that security round the delegates would be relaxed."

"We've got to get back there," said Fisher. "Those poor bastards think they're safe, now I'm not there! They're probably not even bothering with anything more than basic security."

"Let's go," said ap Owen. "Anything could be happening while we're standing around being horrified." He turned to the silently watching Constables. "You stick with us. From now on, you do whatever Hawk and Fisher say. They're in charge. Anyone have any problems with that?" The Guards coughed and shrugged and looked at their boots. Ap Owen smiled slightly. "I thought not. All right, let's move it. Follow me, people."

He led the way out of the inn at a quick, impatient pace, followed resignedly by the Guards. Hawk and Fisher brought up the rear, along with Mistique. Hawk cleared his throat.

"Thanks for the help," he said brusquely. "Of course, we could have beaten the Guards by ourselves, if we'd had to."

"Oh, of course you could, darling," said Mistique. "But you wouldn't have wanted to hurt all those innocent people, would you?"

"Of course not," said Fisher, looking straight ahead. "That's why we were holding back. Otherwise, we could have beaten them easily."

"Of course," said Mistique.

The Peace Talks had ground to a halt yet again, and the four remaining delegates were taking another break in the study. None of them minded much; they all knew nothing important was going to be decided until the new delegates arrived to replace the two who'd died. And in particular, the Haven delegation wasn't going to agree to anything until they had a sorcerer on their side who could counteract any subtle magics the Lord Nightingale might or might not be using to influence things. No one admitted any of this out loud, of course, but everyone understood the situation. They still kept the Talks going. They were, after all, politicians, and there was always the chance someone might be manoeuvred into saying something they hadn't meant to. Careers could be built by pouncing on lapses like that.

Lord Nightingale selected one of the cut-glass decanters and poured out generous measures for them all. The mood was generally more relaxed than it had been, now that the traitor Fisher had been exposed, and they shared little jokes and anecdotes as they emptied their glasses. Nothing like talking for ages and saying nothing to work up a really good thirst. Their murmured conversation wandered aimlessly. None of them were in any particular hurry to get back to the Talks. The chairs were comfortable, the room was pleasantly warm, and in a while it would be time to take a break for dinner anyway.

Lord Nightingale looked at the clock on the mantelpiece, heaved himself out of his chair and left the room on a muttered errand. He shut the door, smiled broadly, and then froze as someone in the hall behind him cleared his throat politely. He looked round sharply, and found himself facing ap Owen and Fisher, someone who by his appearance had to be Hawk, and a woman in sorcerer's black. For a moment Nightingale just stood there, his face and mind utterly blank, and then he drew himself up, and nodded quickly to ap Owen.

"Well done, Captain. You've apprehended the traitor Fisher. I'll see you receive a commendation for this."

Ap Owen stared at him stonily. "I'm afraid that's not why we're here, my lord. It is my duty to inform you that you are under arrest."

"If this is some kind of joke, *Captain,* it's in very bad taste. I shall inform your superiors about this."

Ap Owen continued as if he'd never been interrupted. "We've been here some time, my lord, searching the house. Among your belongings we discovered—"

"You searched my room? How dare you! I have diplomatic immunity from this sort of petty harassment!"

"Among your belongings, hidden inside the handle of one of your trunks, we found a quantity of the super-chacal drug."

"A lot of things made sense, once we found the drug," said Fisher. "We knew the drug tied into the Talks somehow, but we didn't have a connection, until we found you. And once we started looking at you closely, all kinds of things became clear. You gave away the location of the house, because you knew you'd be safe inside the pocket dimension. When that didn't work as well as you'd hoped, you used your sorcery to open a door into the dimension, knowing your sorcery would protect you from the creatures you'd summoned. And of course you were able to close the door once it became clear the creatures were getting out of hand and might pose a threat to you. Finally, you've been subtly using your magic all along, influencing the delegates to make sure nothing would ever be agreed. You've gone very quiet, my lord. Nothing to say for yourself?"

"I admit everything," said Lord Nightingale calmly. "I'll admit anything you like, here, in private. It doesn't matter anymore. You can't prove any of it, and even if you could, I have diplomatic immunity from arrest. And I'm afraid the whole matter is academic now, anyway. My fellow delegates have just drunk a glass of wine from a decanter I dosed rather heavily with the super-chacal drug. My sorcery protected me from suffering any effects, but we should begin to hear the results on them any time now. They'll tear each other to pieces in an animal frenzy, and that will be the end of the Peace Talks. Evidence is already being planted in the right places that this was the work of certain leading factions in Haven, to express their opposition to the thought of peace with Outremer."

"Why?" said Hawk. "Why have you done all this? What sane man wants to start a war?"

Lord Nightingale smiled condescendingly. "There's money to be made in a war, Captain. A great deal of money. Not to mention political capital, and military advancement. A man in the right place at the right time, if properly forewarned, can rise rapidly in wartime, no matter who wins. Whatever the outcome of the war, my associates and I will end up a great deal richer and more powerful than we could ever have hoped to be under normal conditions. The super-chacal was my idea. I helped fund its creation, and oversaw its introduction into Haven. You can think of this city as a testing ground for the new drug. If it does as well here as we expect, it should prove an excellent means of sabotaging the Low Kingdoms. We'll introduce the drug into selected foods and wines, poison some strategic wells and rivers, and then just sit back and watch as your country tears itself apart. All we'll have to do is come in afterwards and clean up the mess. It could be the start of a whole new form of warfare.

"I hope you've all been listening carefully. It's so nice to be appreciated for one's work. And it's not as if you'll ever get a chance to tell anyone else. My fellow delegates should see to that."

He reached to open the study door, and then hesitated, listening. Hawk smiled coldly.

"That's right, my lord. Quiet in there, isn't it? Like ap

Owen said, we've been here for some time. Mistique's magic revealed that one of the decanters had been drugged, so we switched it for another one. The original should make good evidence at your trial. As for your citywide test of the drug, you can forget that, too. We got it all back before it could hit the streets, and it's currently being protected by some very trustworthy Guards. Morgan is dead. So is Burns. You're on your own now, Nightingale."

"You can't arrest me," said Lord Nightingale. "I have diplomatic immunity."

"I think your people can be persuaded to waive that," said Hawk. "You'll be surprised how fast they disown you, to avoid being implicated themselves. After all, no one loves a failure. They'll probably let us hang you right here in Haven, if we ask them nicely."

Lord Nightingale suddenly raised his hands and spoke a Word of Power, and halfway down the hall the air split open. A howling wind came roaring out of the widening split, carrying a rush of thick snow and a bitter blast of cold. Within seconds, a blizzard raged in the narrow hallway, and the temperature plummeted. Ice formed thickly on the doors and walls, and made the floor treacherous underfoot. Hawk raised an arm to protect his face as the freezing wind cut at his exposed skin like a knife. The cold was so intense it burned, and even the shallowest breath was painful.

Hawk glared about him into the swirling snow, trying to locate Lord Nightingale, but he and everyone else had become little more than shadows in the roaring white. From behind him, he could hear something howling in the world beyond the gateway that Nightingale had opened. It sounded huge and angry and utterly inhuman. More howls sounded over the roaring of the blizzard and the buffeting wind, growing louder all the time, and Hawk realised the creatures were slowly drawing nearer. He staggered forward, head bent against the wind, until his flailing arms found the nearest wall. Nightingale would be just as blind in this storm as everyone else, so he had to be following the wall to find his way out. All Hawk had to do was make his way down the wall after him—assuming he hadn't got so turned around in the blizzard that he'd ended up against the wrong wall. . . . Hawk decided he wasn't going to think about that. He had to be right.

And then his heart leapt in his chest as a door suddenly opened to his right, revealing the startled faces of the other delegates. The force of the storm quickly threw them back into the study, where they struggled to close the door again, but Hawk took little notice. He knew now that he'd found the right wall. The howling of the creatures came again, rising eerily over the sound of the storm. They sounded very close. Hawk ran down the corridor, slipping and sliding on the ice, his shoulder pressed against the wall. A shadow loomed up before him. Hawk threw himself forward, grabbed the figure by the shoulder, and slammed it back against the wall. He thrust his face close up against the other's, and smiled savagely as he recognised Nightingale's frightened face.

"We've got to get out of here!" shouted Nightingale, his voice barely audible over the roar of the blizzard. "The creatures will be here soon!"

"I've got a better idea," said Hawk, not caring if the Outremer lord heard him. He took a firm hold of Nightingale's collar and dragged him kicking and struggling back down the corridor towards the gateway he'd opened.

Hawk had to fight the force of the storm with every step, as well as hang on to Nightingale with a hand so numb he could barely feel his grip anymore, and he thought for a while that he wasn't going to make it. But then suddenly he was close enough to make out the split in the air, stretching from floor to ceiling, and he lurched to a halt. The split was wider now. Huge dark shadows moved in the blizzard beyond the gateway. The creatures were almost there. Their howls were deafening. Hawk put his mouth against Nightingale's ear.

"Close the gateway! Close it, or I swear I'll throw you through that opening and let those things have you!"

Nightingale lifted his hands and chanted something, the words lost in the tumult of the blizzard and the creatures' incessant howling. For a long, heart-stopping moment nothing happened, and then the split in the air snapped together and was gone, and the blizzard collapsed. The sudden silence was shocking, and everyone just stood where they were, numbly watching the last of the snow drift lazily on the air before falling to the floor. The corridor seemed a little less cold, but their breath still steamed on the air before them. Nightingale lurched away from Hawk, and headed down the corridor at a shaky run. Hawk caught up with him before he'd gone a dozen paces, and clubbed him from behind with the butt of his axe. Nightingale fell limply into the thick snow on the floor, and lay still. Hawk leaned over him and hit him again, just to be sure. Then he dragged him back to the others. Ap Owen shook his head unhappily.

"They won't let us put him on trial, you know. He'd be an embarrassment to both sides, and probably prevent any future Talks. And besides, diplomatic immunity's too important a concept in troubled times like these. They'll never allow it to be waived, no matter what the crime."

"You mean he's going to get away with it?" said Fisher, scowling dangerously.

Ap Owen shrugged. "Like I said; he's an embarrassment. His own people will probably take away his position and privileges and send him into internal exile, but that's about it."

"Right," said Hawk. "Technically, for what he tried to do, he should be executed, but there's no way that will happen. Aristocrats don't believe in passing death sentences on their own kind if they can avoid it. It might give the peasants ideas." He looked down at Nightingale's unconscious body, his face set and cold. "So many people dead, because of him. All the people who might have died. And I almost raised my axe against Isobel. . . . If I killed him now, no one would say anything. They'd probably even thank me for getting rid of such an embarrassment."

"You can't just kill him in cold blood!" protested ap Owen.

"No," said Hawk finally. "I can't. Even after all these years in Haven, I still know what's right and what's wrong.

I only kill when I have to. I know my duty."

"Look on the bright side," said Mistique cheerfully. "You found the drug before it hit the streets, exposed the traitor in the Guard, and with Nightingale removed from the Talks, they might actually start agreeing on things. You've saved the city and possibly averted a war. What more do you want?"

Hawk and Fisher looked at each other.

"Overtime," said Hawk firmly.

10

Loose Ends

As prisons went, it wasn't too bad. Certainly Lord Nightingale had spent longer periods under far worse conditions during his travels. He'd known some country inns that boasted accommodations so primitive even a leper would have turned up what was left of his nose at them. His present circumstances were surprisingly pleasant, and, all things considered, the Outremer Embassy in Haven had gone out of its way to treat him with every courtesy. He was confined in one of the Embassy's guest rooms, with every comfort the staff could provide, until such time as he could be escorted back to Outremer. And given the current appalling weather conditions, that could be quite some time.

Nightingale didn't mind. The longer the better, as far as he was concerned. He was already filling his time writing carefully worded letters to certain people of standing and influence back in Outremer. There were quite a few who shared his feelings about the coming war, people who could be trusted to see that his case was presented to the King in its most positive light. He'd have to spend some time in internal exile, of course; that was only to be expected. But once the war began, as it inevitably would, and his associates became men of power at Court, he would undoubtedly be summoned again, and his present little setback would be nothing more than an unfortunate memory. In the meantime, his current captors were being very careful to treat him with the utmost respect, for fear of alienating the wrong people. You could always rely on diplomats to appreciate the political realities; particularly when their own careers might be at risk.

So, for the moment, Nightingale bided his time and was the perfect prisoner, never once complaining or making any fuss, and the time passed pleasantly enough. There were books to read and letters to write, and a steady stream of visitors from among the Embassy staff, just stopping by for a chat, and dropping not especially subtle hints of encouragement and support, in the hope of being remembered in the future. True, his door was always locked, and there was an armed guard in the corridor outside his room, but given the current circumstances, Nightingale found that rather reassuring. If word of what he'd intended were to get out in Haven, the populace would quite probably attempt to storm the building and drag him out to hang him from the nearest lamppost. You couldn't expect the rabble to understand the importance of concepts like diplomatic immunity.

There was a sudden knocking at the door, and Nightingale jumped in spite of himself. He cleared his throat carefully, and called for his visitor to enter. A key turned in the lock, and the heavy door swung open to reveal Major de Tournay, carrying a bottle of wine. Nightingale was somewhat surprised to see the Major, but kept all trace of it from his face. De Tournay had taken the news of Nightingale's treachery surprisingly calmly, given that his life had been one of those threatened, but even so he was one of the last people Nightingale had expected to drop by for a chat. Still, recent events had done much to turn up unexpected allies.

"Come in, my dear Major," he said warmly. "Is that wine for me? How splendid." He studied the bottle's label, and raised an appreciative eyebrow. "I'm obliged to you, de Tournay. The Ambassador means well, but his cellar is shockingly depleted."

"I need to talk to you, my lord," said de Tournay bluntly. He looked vaguely round the room, as though embarrassed to be there and unsure how to proceed. Nightingale waved for him to sit down on a chair opposite, and the Major did so, sitting stiffly and almost at attention. "We need to discuss the present situation, my lord. There are matters which need to be . . . clarified."

"Of course, Major. But first, let us sample this excellent wine you've brought me."

De Tournay nodded, and watched woodenly as Nightingale removed the cork, sniffed it, and poured them both a generous glass. They toasted each other politely, but though de Tournay drank deeply, his attention remained fixed on Nightingale rather than the wine.

"Before we begin, Major," said Nightingale, leaning elegantly back in his chair, "perhaps you would oblige me by bringing me up to date on what is happening with Captains Hawk and Fisher. I must confess I half expect every knock at my door to be them, come to drag me off in chains to face Haven justice, or worse still, administer it themselves."

"You needn't worry about them," said de Tournay. "They had their chance to kill you, and chose not to. They understand the realities of the situation. And since they've been cleared of all charges, they're not foolish enough to risk their necks again by harassing you."

"I'm relieved to hear it." Nightingale drank his wine unhurriedly, ignoring de Tournay's impatience to get to the point of his visit. Nightingale smiled. It was very good wine. "Now then, Major, what exactly did you want to see me about?"

"Are there really plans to use this super-chacal drug as a weapon in a war against Haven?"

"Of course. I feel sure it will be very effective. The few test results we've seen have been very promising."

"It's a dishonourable way to fight a war," said de Tournay flatly.

Nightingale laughed, honestly amused. "There's nothing honourable about war, Major. It's nothing but slaughter and destruction on a grand scale, and the more efficiently it's pursued, the better. The drug is just another weapon, that's all."

"But your way leaves no room for heroes or triumphs. Only the spectacle of mad animals, tearing each other to pieces."

Nightingale poured himself another glass of wine, and topped up de Tournay's. "I take it you're one of those people who doesn't want this war, de Tournay. Allow me to remind you that a war is vital if your career is to advance at all. There's no other way for you to gain rank or position so quickly. Or are you content to be a Major all your life?"

"I have ambitions. But I'd prefer to obtain my advances cleanly and honourably."

"Oh, don't worry, Major. There will be plenty of honest slaughter for you and your troops to get involved in. The drug will be used mainly against the civilian population, as a means of destroying morale. You should be grateful, Major. The drug will make your job a great deal easier. Leave policy to the politicians, de Tournay. It's not your province to worry about such things."

De Tournay shrugged. "Maybe you're right." He rose abruptly to his feet, gulped down the last of his wine, and put down the empty glass with unnecessary force. "I'm afraid I can't stay any longer, my lord. Business to attend to. Enjoy your wine." He bowed formally and left, shutting the door quietly behind him.

Nightingale listened to the key turning in the lock, and shrugged. Poor, innocent Major de Tournay. A good judge of wine, though. He raised his glass in a sardonic toast to the closed door.

De Tournay walked unhurriedly down the corridor, and nodded to the bored guard standing at the far end. "The Lord Nightingale doesn't wish to be disturbed for the rest of the afternoon. See to it, would you?"

The guard nodded, and then smiled his thanks at the Major's generous tip. De Tournay made his way through the bustling corridors of the Embassy and out into the packed streets, paying no attention to anyone he passed, lost in his own thoughts. The wine should be taking effect soon. There was a certain ironic justice in Nightingale's falling prey to the very drug he'd championed so highly. It hadn't been too difficult to obtain a small supply of the super-chacal from Guard Headquarters, though procuring an antidote he could take in advance had proved rather expensive. But he'd known he'd have to drink the wine too, so Nightingale wouldn't be suspicious. The drug should be raging through Nightingale's system by now. Left alone, locked in his room, Lord Nightingale would tear himself apart, victim of his own murderous intentions. Which only went to prove there was some justice in the world. You just had to help it along now and again.

De Tournay smiled briefly, and walked off into the city, disappearing into the milling crowds.

Hawk and Fisher stood together outside Guard Headquarters, watching the crowds. They'd been officially cleared of all outstanding charges, officially yelled at for getting themselves into such a mess in the first place by going off on their own, officially congratulated for exposing the traitors Burns and Nightingale, and very officially refused any extra overtime payments. At which point Hawk and Fisher had decided it was time to leave, before things got even more complicated. Hawk thought briefly about apologising to Commander Glen for hitting him, but one look at Glen's simmering glare was enough to convince him it might not be the best time to bring the matter up.

He smiled regretfully, and looked about him. The streets were packed with people trudging determinedly through the snow and slush, none of them paying Hawk and Fisher any attention at all. Hawk grinned. He liked it that way. After everything they'd been through, it made a pleasant change.

"I still can't believe how quickly everyone believed you were crazy and I was a traitor," said Fisher. "When you consider everything we've done for this city . . ."

"Yeah, well," said Hawk. "That's Haven for you. And it has to be said, our reputations didn't help. Half of Haven thinks we're crazy anyway for being so honest, and thinking we can change things, and the other half is scared stiff we're going to kill them on sight."

"We need our reputations; we couldn't get any work done without them. It's still no reason to turn on us like that. You know, Hawk, the more I think about it, the more I think Haven is such a worthless cesspool it's not worth saving. It's crooked and corrupt and so steeped in sin we might have done the Low Kingdoms a favour by just staying out of things and letting Morgan dump his drugs onto the streets."

"Now don't be like that, Isobel. Most people in Haven are just like anyone else in any other city—good people struggling to make ends meet, keep their heads above water, and hold their families together. They're too busy working all the hours God sends to think about making trouble. That's why we do this job; because they're worth protecting from the scum out there who try to steal what little those people have. Most people here are all right."

"Yeah?" growled Fisher. "Name two."

She broke off as a woman wrapped in tattered furs waded through the thick slush to get to them. She was hauling along by one hand a little girl of about five or six, so buried under mismatched furs as to be little more than a bundle on legs. The mother lurched to a halt before Hawk and Fisher and stopped for a moment to get her breath. The little girl looked up at Hawk, smiled shyly, and then hid her face behind her mother's leg. The mother nodded to Fisher, and smiled broadly at Hawk.

"I just wanted to say thank you, Captain. For going down into the rubble after the tenement collapsed, and bringing out my little Katie safe and sound. She'd have died, if it hadn't been for you. Thank you."

Hawk looked down at the little girl, and smiled slowly. "They told me she was dead."

"Bless your heart, no, Captain! Someone found her foot in the rubble, and the doctors stuck it back on with a healing spell! And the Guard is paying the bill! Almost makes you believe in miracles. She's right as rain now. Thanks to you, Captain. I never did believe all the terrible things they say about you."

She plunged forward, hugged him tight, kissed him quickly and stepped back again. She nodded to Fisher and set off down the street, hauling her daughter along behind her. The little girl looked back briefly and waved goodbye, and then mother and child disappeared into the crowd and were gone. Fisher looked at Hawk.

"All right, that's two."